ALEXANDER McCALL SMITH

MORALITY FOR BEAUTIFUL GIRLS

In addition to the huge international phenomenon The No. 1 Ladies' Detective Agency series, Alexander McCall Smith is the author of The Sunday Philosophy Club series, the Portuguese Irregular Verbs series, *The Girl Who Married a Lion*, and *44 Scotland Street*. He was born in what is now Zimbabwe and taught law at the University of Botswana and Edinburgh University. He lives in Scotland and returns regularly to Botswana.

BOOKS BY ALEXANDER MCCALL SMITH

IN THE NO. 1 LADIES' DETECTIVE AGENCY SERIES

The No. 1 Ladies' Detective Agency

Tears of the Giraffe

Morality for Beautiful Girls

The Kalahari Typing School for Men

The Full Cupboard of Life

In the Company of Cheerful Ladies

IN THE SUNDAY PHILOSOPHY CLUB SERIES

The Sunday Philosophy Club

Friends, Lovers, Chocolate

IN THE PORTUGUESE IRREGULAR VERBS SERIES

Portuguese Irregular Verbs

The Finer Points of Sausage Dogs

At the Villa of Reduced Circumstances

The Girl Who Married a Lion and Other Tales of Africa

44 Scotland Street

MORALITY FOR BEAUTIFUL GIRLS

MORALITY FOR BEAUTIFUL GIRLS

Alexander McCall Smith

Anchor Books
A Division of Random House, Inc.
New York

FIRST ANCHOR BOOKS EDITION, NOVEMBER 2002

 Published in the United States by Anchor Books, a division of Random House, Inc., New York, and simultaneously in Canada by Random House of Canada Limited, Toronto. Originally published in softcover in Scotland by Polygon, Edinburgh, in 2001.

Library of Congress Cataloging-in-Publication Data
McCall Smith, R. A.
Morality for beautiful girls / Alexander McCall Smith.
p. cm.
1. Ramotswe, Precious (Fictitious character)—Fiction. 2. Women private investigators—Botswana—Fiction. 3. Beauty contests—Fiction. 4. Botswana—Fiction. I. Title.

PR6063.C326 M67 2002
823'.914—dc21 2002071712

Anchor ISBN 10: 1-4000-3136-2
Anchor ISBN 13: 978-1-4000-3136-8

www.anchorbooks.com

Printed in the United States of America
25 27 29 30 28 26

This book is for
Jean Denison
and
Richard Denison

MORALITY FOR BEAUTIFUL GIRLS

CHAPTER ONE

THE WORLD AS SEEN BY ANOTHER PERSON

MMA RAMOTSWE, the daughter of the late Obed Ramotswe of Mochudi, near Gaborone, Botswana, Africa, was the announced fiancée of Mr J.L.B. Matekoni, son of the late Pumphamilitse Matekoni, of Tlokweng, peasant farmer and latterly chief caretaker of the Railway Head Office. It was a fine match, everybody thought; she, the founder and owner of The No. 1 Ladies' Detective Agency, Botswana's only detective agency for the concerns of both ladies and others; he, the proprietor of Tlokweng Road Speedy Motors, and by general repute one of the finest mechanics in Botswana. It was always a good thing, people said, to have independent interests in a marriage. Traditional marriages, in which the man made all the decisions and controlled most of the household assets, were all very well for women who wanted to spend their time cooking and looking after children, but times had changed, and for educated women who wanted to make something of their lives, it was undoubtedly better for both spouses to have something to do.

There were many examples of such marriages. There was that of Mma Maketetse, for example, who had set up a small factory specialising in the making of khaki shorts for schoolboys. She had started with a cramped and ill-ventilated sewing room at the back of her house, but by employing her cousins to cut and sew for her she had built up one of Botswana's best businesses, exporting khaki shorts to Namibia in the face of stiff competition from large clothing factories in the Cape. She had married Mr Cedric Maketetse, who ran two bottle stores in Gaborone, the capital, and had recently opened a third in Francistown. There had been a faintly embarrassing article about them in the local paper, with the catchy headline: *Shorts manufacturing lady buttons it up with drink merchant.* They were both members of the Chamber of Commerce, and it was clear to all that Mr Maketetse was immensely proud of his wife's business success.

Of course, a woman with a successful business had to be careful that a man who came courting her was not merely looking for a way of spending the rest of his days in comfort. There had been plenty of cases of that happening, and Mma Ramotswe had noticed that the consequences of such unions were almost inevitably dire. The man would either drink or gamble away the profits of his wife's enterprise, or he would try to run the business and destroy it in the process. Men were good at business, thought Mma Ramotswe, but women were just as good. Women were thriftier by nature; they had to be, trying to run households on a tight budget and feed the ever-open mouths of children. Children ate so much, it seemed, and one could never cook enough pumpkin or porridge to fill their hungry bellies. And as for men, they never seemed happier than when eating large quantities of expensive meat. It was all rather discouraging.

"That will be a good marriage," people said, when they heard of her engagement to Mr J.L.B. Matekoni. "He is a reliable man, and she is a very good woman. They will be very happy running their businesses and drinking tea together."

Mma Ramotswe was aware of this popular verdict on her engagement and shared the sentiment. After her disastrous marriage to Note Mokoti, the jazz trumpeter and incorrigible ladies' man, she had decided that she would never remarry, in spite of frequent offers. Indeed, she had initially turned down Mr J.L.B. Matekoni when he had first proposed, only to accept him some six months later. She had realised that the best test of a prospective husband involves no more than the asking of a very simple question, which every woman—or at least every woman who has had a good father—can pose and to which she will know the answer in her bones. She had asked herself this question in respect of Mr J.L.B. Matekoni, and the answer had been unambiguous.

"And what would my late Daddy have thought of him?" she said to herself. She posed the question after she had accepted Mr J.L.B. Matekoni, as one might ask oneself whether one had taken the right turning at a road junction. She remembered where she had been when she asked it. She was taking an evening walk near the dam, along one of those paths that led this way and that through the thorn bushes. She had suddenly stopped, and looked up at the sky, into that faint, washed out blue that would suddenly, at the approach of sunset, become streaked with copper-red. It was a quiet time of the day, and she was utterly alone. And so she spoke the question out loud, as if there were somebody there to hear it.

She looked up at the sky, half-expecting the answer to be there. But of course it was not, and she knew it anyway, without the need to look. There was no doubt in her mind that Obed Ramotswe, who had seen every sort of man during the time he had worked in those distant mines, and who knew the foibles of all of them, would have approved of Mr J.L.B. Matekoni. And if that were the case, then she should have no fears about her future husband. He would be kind to her.

NOW, SITTING in the office of the No. 1 Ladies' Detective Agency with her assistant, Mma Makutsi, the most distinguished graduate of her year at the Botswana Secretarial College, she reflected on the decisions which her impending marriage to Mr J.L.B. Matekoni would oblige her to take. The most immediate issue, of course, had been where they might live. That had been decided rather quickly; Mr J.L.B. Matekoni's house near the old Botswana Defence Club, attractive though it undoubtedly was, with its old colonial verandah and its shiny tin roof, was not as suitable as her own house in Zebra Drive. His garden was sparse; little more than a swept yard, in fact; whereas she had a good collection of paw-paw trees, some very shady acacias, and a well-established melon patch. Moreover, when it came to the interiors, there was little to recommend Mr J.L.B. Matekoni's spartan corridors and unlived-in rooms, especially when compared with the layout of her own house. It would be a great wrench, she felt, to abandon her living room, with its comfortable rug on the red-polished concrete floor, her mantelpiece with her commemorative plate of Sir Sereste Khama, Paramount Chief, Statesman, and first President of Botswana, and, in the corner, her treadle sewing machine that still worked so well, even in a power cut when more modern sewing machines would fall silent.

She had not had to say very much about it. In fact, the decision in favour of Zebra Drive did not even have to be spelled out. After Mr J.L.B. Matekoni had been persuaded by Mma Potokwane, the matron at the orphan farm, to act as foster father to an orphaned boy and his crippled sister, the children had moved into her house and immediately settled in. After that, it was accepted that the whole family would, in due course, live in Zebra Drive. For the time being, Mr J.L.B. Matekoni would continue to live in his own house, but would take his evening meal at Zebra Drive.

That was the easy part of the arrangement. Now there remained the issue of the business. As Mma Ramotswe sat at her desk, watching Mma Makutsi shuffling papers in the filing cabinet of their small office, her thoughts were taken up with the difficult task that lay ahead of her. It had not been an easy decision to make, but she had now made it and she would have to steel herself and put it into effect. That was what business was all about.

One of the most elementary rules of running a business was that facilities should not be needlessly duplicated. After she and Mr J.L.B. Matekoni married, they would have two businesses with two offices. They were very different concerns, of course, but Tlokweng Road Speedy Motors had a large amount of office space and it would make a great deal of sense for Mma Ramotswe to run her agency from there. She had made a close inspection of Mr J.L.B. Matekoni's building and had even obtained advice from a local builder.

"There will be no difficulty," he had said after inspecting the garage and its office. "I can put in a new door on that side over there. Then the clients for your business can come in and not have anything to do with all those greasy goings-on in the workshop."

Combining the two offices would enable Mma Ramotswe to let out her own office and the income derived from that would make all the difference. At present, the uncomfortable truth about the No. 1 Ladies' Detective Agency was that it was simply not making enough money. It was not that there were no clients—there had been a ready supply of those—it was just that detective work was immensely time-consuming and people were simply unable to pay for her services if she charged at a realistic hourly rate. A couple of hundred pula for the resolution of uncertainty or for the finding of a missing person was affordable, and usually well worth it, but several thousand pula for the same job was another matter altogether. Doubt could be preferable to sure knowledge if the difference between the two was a large sum of money.

The business might have broken even if it were not for the wages which Mma Ramotswe had to pay Mma Makutsi. She had originally employed her as a secretary, on the grounds that every business which wished to be taken seriously had to have a secretary, but had soon realised the talents that lay behind those large spectacles. Mma Makutsi had been promoted to assistant detective, a position that gave her the status she so craved. But Mma Ramotswe had felt obliged to raise her pay at the same time, thus plunging the agency's current account further into the red.

She had discussed the matter with Mr J.L.B. Matekoni, who had agreed with her that she had very little choice.

"If you continue like this," he said gravely, "you'll end up bankrupt. I've seen that happen to businesses. They appoint somebody called a judicial manager. He is like a vulture, circling, circling. It is a very bad thing to happen to a business."

Mma Ramotswe clicked her tongue. "I do not want that," she said. "It would be a very sad end to the business."

They had looked at one another glumly. Then Mr J.L.B. Matekoni spoke. "You'll have to sack her," he said. "I've had to sack mechanics in the past. It is not easy, but that is what business is about."

"She was so happy when I promoted her," said Mma Ramotswe quietly. "I can't suddenly tell her that she is no longer a detective. She has no people here in Gaborone. Her people are up in Bobonong. They are very poor, I think."

Mr J.L.B. Matekoni shook his head. "There are many poor people," he said. "Many of these people are suffering badly. But you cannot keep a business going on air. That is well-known. You have to add what you get in and then take away what you spend. The difference is your profit. In your case, there is a minus sign in front of that figure. You cannot . . ."

"I cannot," broke in Mma Ramotswe. "I cannot sack her now. I am like her mother. She wants so much to be a detective and she is hardworking."

Mr J.L.B. Matekoni looked down at his feet. He suspected that Mma Ramotswe was expecting him to propose something, but he was not quite sure what it was. Did she expect him to give her money? Did she want him to meet the bills of the No. 1 Ladies' Detective Agency, even though she had made it so clear that she expected him to keep to his garage business while she attended to her clients and their unsettling problems?

"I do not want you to pay," said Mma Ramotswe, looking at him with a firmness that made him both fear and admire her.

"Of course not," he said hurriedly. "I was not thinking that at all."

"On the other hand," went on Mma Ramotswe, "you do need a secretary at the garage. Your bills are always in a mess, are they not? You never keep a note of what you pay those useless apprentices of yours. I should imagine that you make loans to them, too. Do you keep a record?"

Mr J.L.B. Matekoni looked shifty. How had she found out that the apprentices each owed him over six hundred pula and had shown no signs of being able to repay it?

"Do you want her to come and work for me?" he asked, surprised at the suggestion. "What about her detective position?"

Mma Ramotswe did not answer for a moment. She had not worked anything out, but a plan was now beginning to take shape. If they moved her office to the garage, then Mma Makutsi could keep her job as assistant detective while at the same time she could do the secretarial work that the garage needed. Mr J.L.B. Matekoni could pay her a wage for that, which would mean that the agency's accounts would be relieved of a large part of that burden. This, coupled with the rent which she would receive for the existing offices, would make the financial position look considerably healthier.

She explained her proposal to Mr J.L.B. Matekoni. Although he had always expressed doubts as to Mma Makutsi's usefulness, he could see the attractions of Mma Ramotswe's scheme, not the least of which was that it would keep her happy. And that, he knew, was what he wanted above all else.

MMA RAMOTSWE cleared her throat.

"Mma Makutsi," she began. "I have been thinking about the future."

Mma Makutsi, who had finished her rearranging of the filing cabinet, had made them both a cup of bush tea and was settling down to the half-hour break that she usually took at eleven in the morning. She had started to read a magazine—an old copy of the *National Geographic*—which her cousin, a teacher, had lent her.

"The future? Yes, that is always interesting. But not as interesting as the past, I think. There is a very good article in this magazine, Mma Ramotswe," she said. "I will lend it to you after I have finished reading it. It is all about our ancestors up in East Africa. There is a Dr Leakey there. He is a very famous doctor of bones."

"Doctor of bones?" Mma Ramotswe was puzzled. Mma Makutsi expressed herself very well—both in English and Setswana—but occasionally she used rather unusual expressions. What was a doctor of bones? It sounded rather like a witch doctor, but surely one could not describe Dr Leakey as a witch doctor?

"Yes," said Mma Makutsi. "He knows all about very old bones. He digs them up and tells us about our past. Here, look at this one."

She held up a picture, printed across two pages. Mma Ramotswe squinted to make it out. Her eyes were not what they once were, she had noticed, and she feared that sooner or later she would end up like Mma Makutsi, with her extraordinary, large glasses.

"Is that Dr Leakey?"

Mma Makutsi nodded. "Yes, Mma," she said, "that is him. He is holding a skull which belonged to a very early person. This person lived a long time ago and is very late."

Mma Ramotswe found herself being drawn in. "And this very late person," she said. "Who was he?"

"The magazine says that he was a person when there were very few people about," explained Mma Makutsi. "We all lived in East Africa then."

"Everybody?"

"Yes. Everybody. My people. Your people. All people. We all come from the same small group of ancestors. Dr Leakey has proved that."

Mma Ramotswe was thoughtful. "So we are all brothers and sisters, in a sense?"

"We are," said Mma Makutsi. "We are all the same people. Eskimos, Russians, Nigerians. They are the same as us. Same blood. Same DNA."

"DNA?" asked Mma Ramotswe. "What is that?"

"It is something which God used to make people," explained Mma Makutsi. "We are all made up of DNA and water."

Mma Ramotswe considered the implications of these revelations for a moment. She had no views on Eskimos and Russians, but Nigerians were a different matter. But Mma Makutsi was right, she reflected: if universal brotherhood—and sisterhood—meant anything, it would have to embrace the Nigerians as well.

"If people knew this," she said, "if they knew that we were all from the same family, would they be kinder to one another, do you think?"

Mma Makutsi put down the magazine. "I'm sure they would," she said. "If they knew that, then they would find it very difficult to do unkind things to others. They might even want to help them a bit more."

Mma Ramotswe was silent. Mma Makutsi had made it difficult to go on, but she and Mr J.L.B. Matekoni had taken the decision and she had no alternative but to break the bad news.

"That is all very interesting," she said, trying to sound firm. "I must read more about Dr Leakey when I have more time. At the moment I am having to spend all my time on working out how to keep this business going. The accounts are not good, you know. Our accounts are not like those accounts you see published in the newspapers—you know the ones, where they have two columns, income and expenditure, and the first is always bigger than the second. With this business it is the other way round."

She paused, watching the effect of her words on Mma Makutsi. It was difficult to tell what she was thinking, with those glasses.

"So I am going to have to do something," she went on. "If I do nothing, then we shall be put under judicial management or the bank manager will come and take the office from us. That is what happens to businesses that do not make a profit. It is very bad."

Mma Makutsi was staring at her desk. Then she looked up at Mma Ramotswe and for a moment the branches of the thorn tree outside the window were reflected in her glasses.

Mma Ramotswe found this disconcerting; it was as if one were looking at the world as seen by another person. As she thought this, Mma Makutsi moved her head, and Mma Ramotswe saw, for a moment, the reflection of her own red dress.

"I am doing my best," said Mma Makutsi quietly. "I hope that you will give me a chance. I am very happy being an assistant detective here. I do not want to be just a secretary for the rest of my life."

She stopped and looked at Mma Ramotswe. What was it like, thought Mma Ramotswe, to be Mma Makutsi, graduate of the Botswana Secretarial College with 97 percent in the final examination, but with nobody, except for some people far away up in Bobonong? She knew that Mma Makutsi sent them money, because she had seen her once in the Post Office, buying a postal order for one hundred pula. She imagined that they had been told about the promotion and were proud of the fact that their niece, or whatever she was to them, was doing so well in Gaborone. Whereas the truth was that the niece was being kept as an act of charity and it was really Mma Ramotswe supporting those people up in Bobonong.

Her gaze shifted to Mma Makutsi's desk, and to the still-exposed picture of Dr Leakey holding the skull. Dr Leakey was looking out of the photograph, directly at her. Well Mma Ramotswe? he seemed to be saying. What about this assistant of yours?

She cleared her throat. "You must not worry," she said. "You will still be assistant detective. But we will need you to do some other duties as well when we move over to Tlokweng Road Speedy Motors. Mr J.L.B. Matekoni needs help with his paperwork. Half of you will be a secretary, but half of you will be an assistant detective." She paused, and then added hurriedly, "But you can call yourself assistant detective. That will be your official title."

For the rest of the day, Mma Makutsi was quieter than usual. She made Mma Ramotswe her afternoon tea in silence, handing the mug over to her without saying anything, but at the end of the day she seemed to have accepted her fate.

"I suppose that Mr J.L.B. Matekoni's office is a mess," she said. "I cannot see him doing his paperwork properly. Men do not like that sort of thing."

Mma Ramotswe was relieved by the change of tone. "It is a real mess," she said. "You will be doing him a very good service if you sort it out."

"We were taught how to do that at college," said Mma Makutsi. "They sent us one day to an office that was in a very bad way, and we had to sort it out. There were four of us—myself and three pretty girls. The pretty girls spent all their time talking to the men in the office while I did the work."

"Ah!" said Mma Ramotswe. "I can imagine that."

"I worked until eight o'clock at night," went on Mma Makutsi. "The other girls all went off with the men to a bar at five o'clock and left me there. The next morning, the Principal of the College said that we had all done a very good job and that we were all going to get a top mark for the assignment. The other girls were very pleased. They said that although I had done most of the tidying they had had the more difficult part of the job, which was keeping the men from getting in the way. They really thought that."

Mma Ramotswe shook her head. "They are useless girls, those girls," she said. "There are too many people like that in

Botswana these days. But at least you know that you have succeeded. You are an assistant detective and what are they? Nothing, I should think."

Mma Makutsi took off her large spectacles and polished the lenses carefully with the corner of a handkerchief.

"Two of them are married to very rich men," she said. "They have big houses over near the Sun Hotel. I have seen them walking about in their expensive sunglasses. The third went off to South Africa and became a model. I have seen her picture in a magazine. She has got a husband who is a photographer for that magazine. He has plenty of money too and she is very happy. They call him Polaroid Khumalo. He is very handsome and well-known."

She replaced her glasses and looked at Mma Ramotswe.

"There will be a husband for you some day," said Mma Ramotswe. "And that man will be a very fortunate man."

Mma Makutsi shook her head. "I do not think there will be a husband," she said. "There are not enough men in Botswana. That is a well-known fact. All the men are married now and there is nobody left."

"Well, you don't have to get married," said Mma Ramotswe. "Single girls can have a very good life these days. I am single. I am not married."

"But you are marrying Mr J.L.B. Matekoni," said Mma Makutsi. "You will not be single for long. You could . . ."

"I didn't have to marry him," interrupted Mma Ramotswe. "I was happy by myself. I could have stayed that way."

She stopped. She noticed that Mma Makutsi had taken her spectacles off again and was polishing them once more. They had misted over.

Mma Ramotswe thought for a moment. She had never been

able to see unhappiness and not do something about it. It was a difficult quality for a private detective to have, as there was so much unhappiness entailed in her work, but she could not harden her heart, however much she tried. "Oh, and there's another thing," she said. "I didn't tell you that in this new job of yours you will be described as Assistant Manager of Tlokweng Road Speedy Motors. It is not just a secretarial job."

Mma Makutsi looked up and smiled.

"That is very good," she said. "You are very kind to me, Mma."

"And there will be more money," said Mma Ramotswe, throwing caution aside. "Not much more, but a little bit more. You will be able to send a bit more up to those people of yours up in Bobonong."

Mma Makutsi appeared considerably cheered by this information, and there was a zest in the way in which she performed the last tasks of the day, the typing of several letters which Mma Ramotswe had drafted in longhand. It was Mma Ramotswe who now seemed morose. It was Dr Leakey's fault, she decided. If he had not come into the conversation, then she might have been firmer. As it was, not only had she promoted Mma Makutsi again, but she had given her, without consulting Mr J.L.B. Matekoni, a pay raise. She would have to tell him about that, of course, but perhaps not just yet. There was always a time for the breaking of difficult news, and one had to wait for one's moment. Men usually let their defences down now and then, and the art of being a successful woman, and beating men at their own game, was to wait your moment. When that moment arrived, you could manipulate a man with very little difficulty. But you had to wait.

CHAPTER TWO

A BOY IN THE NIGHT

THEY WERE camped in the Okavango, outside Maun, under a covering of towering mopani trees. To the north, barely half a mile away, the lake stretched out, a ribbon of blue in the brown and green of the bush. The savannah grass here was thick and rich, and there was good cover for the animals. If you wanted to see elephant, you had to be watchful, as the lushness of the vegetation made it difficult to make out even their bulky grey shapes as they moved slowly through their forage.

The camp, which was a semipermanent collection of five or six large tents pitched in a semicircle, belonged to a man they knew as Rra Pula, Mr Rain, owing to the belief, empirically verified on many an occasion, that his presence brought much-needed rain. Rra Pula was happy to allow this belief to be perpetuated. Rain was good luck; hence the cry Pula! Pula! Pula! when good fortune was being celebrated or invoked. He was a thin-faced man with the leathery, sun-speckled skin of the white person who has spent all his life under an African sun. The freckles and sun-spots had now become one, which had made him brown all over, like a pale biscuit put into the oven.

"He is slowly becoming like us," one of his men said as they sat round the fire one night. "One day he will wake up and he will be a Motswana, same colour as us."

"You cannot make a Motswana just by changing his skin," said another. "A Motswana is a Motswana inside. A Zulu is the same as us outside, but inside he is always a Zulu. You can't make a Zulu into a Motswana either. They are different."

There was silence round the fire as they mulled over this issue.

"There are a lot of things that make you what you are," said one of the trackers at last. "But the most important thing is your mother's womb. That is where you get the milk that makes you a Motswana or a Zulu. Motswana milk, Motswana child. Zulu milk, Zulu child."

"You do not get milk in the womb," said one of the younger men. "It is not like that."

The older man glared at him. "Then what do you eat for the first nine months, Mr Clever, Mr BSc? Are you saying that you eat the mother's blood? Is that what you are saying?"

The younger man shook his head. "I am not sure what you eat," he said. "But you do not get milk until you are born. I am certain of that."

The older man looked scornful. "You know nothing. You have no children, have you? What do you know about it? A man with no children talking about children as if he had many. I have five children. Five."

He held up the fingers of one hand. "Five children," he repeated. "And all five were made by their mother's milk."

They fell silent. At the other fire, on chairs rather than logs, were sitting Rra Pula and his two clients. The sound of their voices, unintelligible mumbling, had drifted across to the men, but now they were silent. Suddenly Rra Pula stood up.

"There's something out there," he said. "A jackal maybe. Sometimes they come quite close to the fire. The other animals keep their distance."

One of the clients, a middle-aged man wearing a wide-brimmed slouch hat, stood up and stared into the darkness.

"Would a leopard come in this close?" he asked.

"Never," said Rra Pula. "Very shy creatures."

A woman sitting on a canvas folding stool now turned her head sharply.

"There's definitely something there," she said. "Listen."

Rra Pula put down the mug he had been holding and called across to his men.

"Simon! Motopi! One of you bring me a torch. Double quick!"

The younger man stood up and walked quickly over to the equipment tent. As he walked across to give it to his employer, he too heard the noise and he switched on the powerful light, sweeping its beam through the circle of darkness around the camp. They saw the shapes of the bushes and small trees, all curiously flat and one-dimensional in the probing beam of light.

"Won't that scare it away?" asked the woman.

"Might do," said Rra Pula. "But we don't want any surprises, do we?"

The light swung round and briefly moved up to illuminate

the leaves of a thorn tree. Then it dropped to the base of the tree, and that is where they saw it.

"It's a child," said the man in the slouch hat. "A child? Out here?"

The child was on all fours. Caught in the beam of light, he was like an animal in the headlights of a car, frozen in indecision.

"Motopi!" called Rra Pula. "Fetch that child. Bring him here."

The man with the torch moved quickly through the grass, keeping the beam of light on the small figure. When he reached him, the child suddenly moved sharply back into the darkness, but something appeared to slow him down, and he stumbled and fell. The man reached forward, dropping the torch as he did so. There was a sharp sound as it hit a rock and the light went out. But the man had the child by then, and had lifted him up, kicking and wriggling.

"Don't fight me, little one," he said in Setswana. "I'm not going to hurt you. I'm not going to hurt you."

The child kicked out and his foot caught the man in his stomach.

"Don't do that!" He shook the child, and, holding him with one hand, slapped him hard across the shoulder.

"There! That's what you'll get if you try to kick your uncle! And there'll be more if you don't watch out!"

The child, surprised by the blow, stopped resisting, and went limp.

"And here's another thing," muttered the man, as he walked over towards Rra Pula's fire. "You smell."

He put the boy down on the ground, beside the table where the Tilley lamp stood; but he still held on to the child's wrist, in case he should try to run away or even to kick one of the white people.

"So this is our little jackal," said Rra Pula, looking down at the boy.

"He's naked," said the woman. "He hasn't got a scrap of clothing."

"What age is he?" asked one of the men. "He can't be more than six or seven. At the most."

Rra Pula now lifted up the lamp and held it closer to the child, playing the light over a skin which seemed criss-crossed with tiny scars and scratches, as if he had been dragged through a thorn bush. The stomach was drawn in, and the ribs showed; the tiny buttocks contracted and without flesh; and on one foot, stretching right across the arch, an open sore, white rimmed about a dark centre.

The boy looked up into the light and seemed to draw back from the inspection.

"Who are you?" asked Rra Pula in Setswana. "Where have you come from?"

The child stared at the light, but did not react to the question.

"Try in Kalanga," Rra Pula said to Motopi. "Try Kalanga, then try Herero. He could be Herero. Or a Mosarwa. You can make yourself understood in these languages, Motopi. You see if you can get anything out of him."

The man dropped to his haunches so as to be at the child's level. He started in one language, enunciating the words carefully, and then, getting no reaction, moved to another. The boy remained mute.

"I do not think this child can speak," he said. "I think that he does not know what I am saying."

The woman moved forward and reached out to touch the child's shoulder.

"You poor little thing," she said. "You look as if . . ."

She gave a cry and withdrew her hand sharply. The boy had bitten her.

The man snatched at the child's right arm and dragged him to his feet. Then, leaning forward, he struck him sharply across the face. "No," he shouted. "Bad child!"

The woman, outraged, pushed the man away. "Don't hit him," she cried. "He's frightened. Can't you see? He didn't mean to hurt me. I shouldn't have tried to touch him."

"You cannot have a child biting people, Mma," said the man quietly. "We do not like that."

The woman had wrapped a handkerchief around her hand, but a small blood stain had seeped through.

"I'll get you some penicillin for that," said Rra Pula. "A human bite can go bad."

They looked down at the child, who had now lain down, as if preparing for sleep, but was looking up at them, watching them.

"The child has a very strange smell," said Motopi. "Have you noticed that, Rra Pula?"

Rra Pula sniffed. "Yes," he said. "Maybe it's that wound. It's suppurating."

"No," said Motopi. "I have a very good nose. I can smell that wound, but there is another smell too. It is a smell that you do not find on a child."

"What's that?" asked Rra Pula. "You recognise that smell?"

Motopi nodded. "Yes," he said. "It is the smell of a lion. There is nothing else that has that smell. Only lion."

For a moment nobody said anything. Then Rra Pula laughed.

"Some soap and water will sort all that out," he said. "And something on that sore on his foot. Sulphur powder should dry it out."

Motopi picked up the child, gingerly. The boy stared at him, and cowered, but did not resist.

"Wash him and then keep him in your tent," said Rra Pula. "Don't let him escape."

The clients returned to their seats about the fire. The woman exchanged glances with the man, who lifted an eyebrow and shrugged.

"Where on earth has he come from?" she asked Rra Pula, as he poked at the fire with a charred stick.

"One of the local villages, I expect," he said. "The nearest one is about twenty miles over that way. He's probably a herd boy who got lost and wandered off into the bush. That happens from time to time."

"But why has he got no clothes?"

He shrugged. "Sometimes the herd boys just wear a small apron. He probably lost his to a thorn bush. Perhaps he left it lying somewhere."

He looked up at the woman. "These things happen a lot in Africa. There are plenty of children who go missing. They turn up. No harm comes to them. You aren't worried about him, are you?"

The woman frowned. "Of course I am. Anything could have happened to him. What about the wild animals? He could have been taken by a lion. Anything could have happened to him."

"Yes," said Rra Pula. "It could. But it didn't. We'll take him tomorrow into Maun and leave him with the police down there. They can sort it out. They'll work out where he's come from and get him home."

The woman seemed thoughtful. "Why did your man say that he smelled like a lion? Wasn't that rather an odd thing to say?"

Rra Pula laughed. "People say all sorts of odd things up here. They see things differently. That man, Motopi, is a very good tracker. But he tends to talk about animals as if they were human beings. He says that they say things to him. He claims that he can smell an animal's fear. That's the way he talks. It just is."

They sat in silence for a while, and then the woman announced that she was going to bed. They said good-night, and Rra Pula and the man sat by the fire for another half hour or so, saying very little, watching the logs slowly burn out and the sparks fly up into the sky. Inside his tent, Motopi lay still, stretched out across the entrance so that the child could not get out without disturbing him. But the child was not likely to do that; he had fallen asleep more or less immediately after being put into the tent. Now Motopi, on the verge of drifting off to sleep, watched him through one, heavy-lidded eye. The child, a light kaross thrown over him, was breathing deeply. He had eaten the piece of meat they had given him, ripping at it greedily, and had eagerly drunk the large cup of water which they had offered him, licking at the water as an animal might do at a drinking hole. There was still that strange smell, he thought, that musty-acrid smell which reminded him so strongly of the smell of a lion. But why, he wondered, would a child smell of a lion?

CHAPTER THREE

GARAGE AFFAIRS

ON HER way to Tlokweng Road Speedy Motors, Mma Ramotswe had decided that she would simply have to make a clean breast of it to Mr J.L.B. Matekoni. She knew that she had exceeded her authority by promoting Mma Makutsi to be Assistant Manager of the garage—she would have resented it greatly if he had attempted to promote her own staff—and she realised that she would just have to tell him exactly what had happened. He was a kind man, and although he had always thought that Mma Makutsi was a luxury whom Mma Ramotswe could ill afford, he would surely understand how important it was for her to have a position. After all, it would make no difference if Mma Makutsi called herself Assistant Manager, provided that she was doing the work that she was meant to do. But then there was the problem of the raise in pay. That would be more difficult.

Later that afternoon, driving in the tiny white van which Mr J.L.B. Matekoni had recently fixed for her, Mma Ramotswe made her way to Tlokweng Road Speedy Motors. The van was performing well now that Mr J.L.B. Matekoni spent so much of his spare time tinkering with its engine. He had replaced many of its parts with brand new spares which he had ordered from over the border. There was a new carburettor, for example, and an entirely new set of brakes. Mma Ramotswe now had to do no more than touch the brake pedal and the van would screech to a halt. In the past, before Mr J.L.B. Matekoni had taken such an interest in her van, Mma Ramotswe had been obliged to pump the brake pedal three or four times before she even began to slow down.

"I think I shall never again go into the back of somebody," said Mma Ramotswe gratefully when she tried the new brakes for the first time. "I shall be able to stop exactly when I want to."

Mr J.L.B. Matekoni looked alarmed. "It is very important to have good brakes," he said. "You mustn't let your brakes get like that again. Just you ask me, and I shall make sure that they are in tip-top order."

"I shall do that," Mma Ramotswe promised. She had very little interest in cars, although she dearly loved her tiny white van, which had served her so faithfully. She could not understand why people spent so much time hankering after a Mercedes-Benz when there were many other cars which safely transported one to one's destination, and back again, without requiring a fortune to do so. This interest in cars was a male problem, she thought. One saw it develop in small boys, with the little wire models they made of cars, and it never really went away. Why should men find cars so interesting? A car was no more than a machine, and one might think that men would be interested in washing machines or irons, for that matter. Yet they were not. You never saw men standing around talking about washing machines.

She drove up to the front of Tlokweng Road Speedy Motors and alighted from the tiny white van. Through the small window that gave on to the forecourt, she could see that there was nobody in the office, which meant that Mr J.L.B. Matekoni would probably be under a car in the workshop, or standing over his two difficult apprentices while he attempted to convey to them some difficult point of mechanics. He had confessed to Mma Ramotswe his despair of making anything of these boys, and she had sympathised with him. It was not easy trying to persuade young people of the need to work; they expected everything to be handed to them on a plate. None of them seemed to understand that everything they had in Botswana—and it was a great deal—had been acquired through hard work and self-denial. Botswana had never borrowed money and then sunk into debt as had happened in so many other countries in Africa. They had saved and saved and spent money very carefully; every cent, every thebe, had been accounted for; none had gone into the pockets of politicians. We can be proud of our country, thought Mma Ramotswe; and I am. I'm proud of what my father, Obed Ramotswe did; I'm proud of Seretse Khama and of how he invented a new country out of a place that had been ignored by the British. They may not have cared much about us, she reflected, but now they know what we can do. They admired us for that; she had read what the American Ambassador had said. "We salute the people of Botswana for what they have done," he had announced. The words had made her glow with pride. She knew that people overseas, people in those distant, rather frightening countries, thought highly of Botswana.

It was a good thing to be an African. There were terrible things that happened in Africa, things that brought shame and despair when one thought about them, but that was not all there was in Africa. However great the suffering of the people of Africa, however harrowing the cruelty and chaos brought about by soldiers—small boys with guns, really—there was still so much in Africa from which one could take real pride. There was the kindness, for example, and the ability to smile, and the art and the music.

She walked round to the workshop entrance. There were two cars inside, one up on the ramp, and the other parked against a wall, its battery connected to a small charger by the front wheel. Several parts had been left lying on the floor—an exhaust pipe and another part which she did not recognise—and there was an open toolbox underneath the car on the ramp. But there was no sign of Mr J.L.B. Matekoni.

It was only when one of them stood up that Mma Ramotswe realised that the apprentices were there. They had been sitting on the ground, propped up against an empty oil drum, playing the traditional stone game. Now one of them, the taller boy whose name she could never remember, rose and wiped his hands on his dirty overall.

"Hallo, Mma," he said. "He is not here. The boss. He's gone home."

The apprentice grinned at her in a way which she found slightly offensive. It was a familiar grin, of the sort that one might imagine him giving a girl at a dance. She knew these young men. Mr J.L.B. Matekoni had told her that all they were interested in was girls, and she could well believe it. And the distressing thing was that there would be plenty of girls who would be interested in these young men, with their heavily pomaded hair and their flashing white grins.

"Why has he gone home so early?" she asked. "Is the work all finished? Is that why you two are sitting about?"

The apprentice smiled. He had the air, she thought, of somebody who knew something, and she wondered what it was. Or was it just his sense of superiority, the condescending manner that he probably adopted towards all women?

"No," he replied, glancing down at his friend. "Anything but finished. We still have to deal with that vehicle up there." He gestured casually towards the car on the ramp.

Now the other apprentice arose. He had been eating something and there was a thin line of flour about his mouth. What would the girls think of that? thought Mma Ramotswe mischievously. She imagined him turning on his charm for some girl, blissfully unaware of the flour round his mouth. He may be good-looking, but a white outline around the lips would bring laughter rather than any racing of the heart.

"The boss is often away these days," said the second apprentice. "Sometimes he goes off at two o'clock. He leaves us to do all the work."

"But there's a problem," chipped in the other apprentice. "We can't do everything. We're pretty good with cars, you know, but we haven't learned everything, you know."

Mma Ramotswe glanced up at the car on the ramp. It was one of those old French station wagons which were so popular in parts of Africa.

"That one's an example," said the first apprentice. "It's making steam out of its exhaust. It comes up in a big cloud. That means that a gasket has gone and that the coolant's getting into the piston chamber. So that makes steam. Hiss. Lots of steam."

"Well," said Mma Ramotswe, "why don't you fix it? Mr J.L.B. Matekoni can't hold your hand all the time, you know."

The younger apprentice pouted. "You think that it's simple, Mma? You think it's simple? You ever tried to take the cylinder head off a Peugeot? Have you done that, Mma?"

Mma Ramotswe made a calming gesture. "I was not criticising you," she said. "Why don't you get Mr J.L.B. Matekoni to show you what to do?"

The older apprentice looked irritated. "That's all very well, Mma. But the trouble is that he won't. And then he goes off home and leaves us to explain to the customers. They don't like it. They say: Where's my car? How do you expect me to get around if you're going to take days and days to fix my car? Am I to walk, like a person with no car? That's what they say, Mma."

Mma Ramotswe said nothing for a moment. It seemed so unlikely that Mr J.L.B. Matekoni, who was normally so punctilious, would allow this to happen in his own business. He had built his reputation on getting repairs done well, and speedily. If anybody was dissatisfied with a job that he had done, they were fully entitled to bring the car back and he would do the whole thing again without charge. That was the way that he had always worked, and it seemed inconceivable that he would leave a car up on the ramp in the care of these two apprentices who seemed to know so little about engines and who could not be trusted not to take shortcuts.

She decided to press the older apprentice a bit further. "Do you mean to tell me," she said, her voice lowered, "do you mean to tell me that Mr J.L.B. Matekoni doesn't *care* about these cars?"

The apprentice stared at her, rudely allowing their eyes to lock. If he knew anything about proper behaviour, thought Mma Ramotswe, he wouldn't keep eye contact with me; he would look down, as befits a junior in the presence of a senior.

"Yes," said the apprentice simply. "For the last ten days or so, Mr J.L.B. Matekoni seems to have lost interest in this garage. Only yesterday he told me that he thought he would go away to his village and that I should be left in charge. He said I should do my best."

Mma Ramotswe drew in her breath. She could tell that the young man was telling the truth, but it was a truth which was very difficult to believe.

"And here's another thing," said the apprentice, wiping his hands on a piece of oil rag. "He hasn't paid the spare parts supplier for two months. They telephoned the other day, when he had gone away early, and I took the call, didn't I, Siletsi?"

The other apprentice nodded.

"Anyway," he went on. "Anyway, they said that unless we paid within ten days they would not provide us with any further spare parts. They said that I should tell that to Mr J.L.B. Matekoni and get him to buck up his ways. That's what they said. Me tell the boss. That's what they said I should do."

"And did you?" asked Mma Ramotswe.

"I did," he said. "I said: A word in your ear, Rra. Just a word. Then I told him."

Mma Ramotswe watched his expression. It was clear that he was pleased to be cast in the role of the concerned employee, a role, she suspected, which he had not had occasion to occupy before.

"And then? What did he say to your advice?"

The apprentice sniffed, wiping his hand across his nose.

"He said that he would try to do something about it. That's what he said. But you know what I think? You know what I think is happening, Mma?"

Mma Ramotswe looked at him expectantly.

He went on, "I think that Mr J.L.B. Matekoni has stopped caring about this garage. I think that he has had enough. I think he wants to hand it over to us. Then he wants to go off to his lands out there and grow melons. He is an old man now, Mma. He has had enough."

Mma Ramotswe drew in her breath. The sheer effrontery of the suggestion astonished her: here was this . . . this *useless* apprentice, best known for his ability to pester the girls who walked past the garage, the very apprentice whom Mr J.L.B. Matekoni had once seen using a hammer on an engine, now saying that Mr J.L.B. Matekoni himself was ready to retire.

It took her the best part of a minute to compose herself sufficiently to reply.

"You are a very rude young man," she said at last. "Mr J.L.B. Matekoni has not lost interest in his garage. And he is not an old man. He is just in his early forties, which is not old at all, whatever you people think. And finally, he has no intention of handing the garage over to you two. That would be the end of the business. Do you understand me?"

The older of the apprentices looked for reassurance from his friend, but the other was staring fixedly at the ground.

"I understand you, Mma. I am sorry."

"As well you should be," said Mma Ramotswe. "And here's a bit of news for you. Mr J.L.B. Matekoni has just appointed an assistant manager for this garage. This new manager will be starting here very soon, and you two had better look out."

Her remarks had the desired effect on the older apprentice, who dropped his oily piece of cloth and looked anxiously at the other.

"When does he start?" he asked nervously.

"Next week," said Mma Ramotswe. "And it's a she."

"A she? A woman?"

"Yes," said Mma Ramotswe, turning to leave. "It is a woman called Mma Makutsi, and she is very strict with apprentices. So there will be no more sitting around playing stones. Do you understand?"

The apprentices nodded glumly.

"Then get on with trying to fix that car," said Mma Ramotswe. "I shall come back in a couple of hours and see how it's going."

She walked back to the van and climbed into the driving seat. She had succeeded in *sounding* very determined when she gave the apprentices their instructions, but she felt far from certain inside. In fact, she felt extremely concerned. In her experience, when people began to behave out of character it was a sign that something was very wrong. Mr J.L.B. Matekoni was a thoroughly conscientious man, and thoroughly conscientious men did not let their customers down unless there was a very good reason. But what was it? Was it something to do with their impending marriage? Had he changed his mind? Did he wish to escape?

* * *

MMA MAKUTSI locked the door of the No. 1 Ladies' Detective Agency. Mma Ramotswe had gone off to the garage to talk to Mr J.L.B. Matekoni and had left her to finish the letters and get them to the post. No request made of her would have seemed excessive, so great was Mma Makutsi's joy at her promotion and the news of her increase in wages. It was a Thursday, and tomorrow was payday, even if it would be a payday at the old rate. She would treat herself to something in anticipation, she thought—perhaps a doughnut on the way home. Her route took her past a small stall that sold doughnuts and other fried foods and the smell was tantalising. Money was the problem, though. A large, fried doughnut cost two pula, which made it an expensive treat, especially if one thought what the evening meal would cost. Living in Gaborone was expensive; everything seemed to cost twice as much as it did at home. In the country, ten pula would get one a long way; here in Gaborone ten pula notes seemed to melt in one's hand.

Mma Makutsi rented a room in the backyard of a house off the Lobatse Road. The room formed half of a small, breeze-block shack which looked out to the back fence and a meandering lane, the haunt of thin-faced dogs. The dogs were loosely attached to the people who lived in the houses, but seemed to prefer their own company and roamed about in packs of two or three. Somebody must have fed them, at irregular intervals, but their rib cages still showed and they seemed constantly to be scavenging for scraps from the rubbish bins. On occasion, if Mma Makutsi left her door open, one of these dogs would wander in and gaze at her with mournful, hungry eyes until she shooed it out. This was perhaps a greater indignity than that which befell her at work, when the chickens came into the office and started pecking about her feet.

She bought her doughnut at the stall and ate it there and then, licking the sugar off her fingers when she had finished. Then, her hunger assuaged, she began the walk home. She could have ridden home in a minibus—it was a cheap enough form of transport—but she enjoyed the walk in the cool of the evening, and she was usually in no hurry to reach home. She wondered how he was; whether it had been a good day for her brother, or whether his coughing would have tired him out. He had been quite comfortable over the last few days, although he was very weak now, and she had enjoyed one or two nights of unbroken sleep.

He had come to live with her two months earlier, making the long journey from their home by bus. She had gone to meet him at the bus station down by the railway, and for a brief moment she had looked at him without recognising him. The last time she had seen him he had been well-built, even bulky; now he was stooped and thin and his shirt flapped loosely about his torso. When she realised that it was him, she had run up and taken his hand, which had shocked her, for it was hot and dry and the skin was cracked. She had lifted his suitcase for him, although he had tried to do that himself, and had carried it all the way to the minibus that plied its trade down the Lobatse Road.

After that, he had settled in, sleeping on the mat which she had set up on the other side of her room. She had strung a wire from wall to wall and hung a curtain over it, to give him privacy and some sense of having his own place, but she heard every rasping breath he drew and was often woken by his mumbling in his dreams.

"You are a kind sister to take me in," he said. "I am a lucky man to have a sister like you."

She had protested that it was no trouble, and that she liked having him with her, and that he could stay with her when he was better and found a job in Gaborone, but she knew that this was not going to happen. He knew too, she was sure, but neither spoke about it or the cruel disease which was ending his life, slowly, like a drought dries up a landscape.

Now, coming home, she had good news for him. He was always very interested to hear what had happened at the agency, as he always asked her for all the details of her day. He had never met Mma Ramotswe—Mma Makutsi did not want her to know about his illness—but he had a very clear picture of her in his head and he always asked after her.

"I will meet her one day, maybe," he said. "And I will be able to thank her for what she has done for my sister. If it hadn't been for her, then you would never have been able to become an assistant detective."

"She is a kind woman."

"I know she is," he said. "I can see this nice woman with her smile and her fat cheeks. I can see her drinking tea with you. I am happy just to think about it."

Mma Makutsi wished that she had thought to buy him a doughnut, but often he had no appetite and it would have been wasted. His mouth was painful, he said, and the cough made it difficult for him to eat very much. So often he would take only a few spoonfuls of the soup which she prepared on her small paraffin stove, and even then he would sometimes have difficulty in keeping these down.

Somebody else was in the room when she got home. She heard a strange voice and for a moment she feared that something terrible had happened in her absence, but when she entered the room she saw that the curtain had been drawn back and that there was a woman sitting on a small folding stool beside his mat. When she heard the door open, the woman stood up and turned to face her.

"I am the nurse from the Anglican hospice," she said. "I have come to see our brother. My name is Sister Baleje."

The nurse had a pleasant smile, and Mma Makutsi took to her immediately.

"You are kind to come and see him," Mma Makutsi said. "I wrote that letter to you just to let you know that he was not well."

The nurse nodded. "That was the right thing to do. We can call in to see him from time to time. We can bring food if you need it. We can do something to help, even if it's not a great deal. We have some drugs we can give him. They are not very strong, but they can help a bit."

Mma Makutsi thanked her, and looked down at her brother.

"It is the coughing that troubles him," she said. "That is the worst thing, I think."

"It is not easy," said the nurse.

The nurse sat down on her stool again and took the brother's hand.

"You must drink more water, Richard," she said. "You must not let yourself get too thirsty."

He opened his eyes and looked up at her, but said nothing. He was not sure why she was here, but thought that she was a friend of his sister, perhaps, or a neighbour.

The nurse looked at Mma Makutsi and gestured for her to sit on the floor beside them. Then, still holding his hand, she reached forward and gently touched his cheek.

"Lord Jesus," she said, "who helps us in our suffering. Look down on this poor man and have mercy on him. Make his days joyful. Make him happy for his good sister here, who looks after him in his illness. And bring him peace in his heart."

Mma Makutsi closed her eyes, and put her hand on the shoulder of the nurse, where it rested, as they sat in silence.

CHAPTER FOUR

A VISIT TO DR MOFFAT

AS MMA Makutsi sat at her brother's side, Mma Ramotswe was driving her tiny white van up to the gate of Mr J.L.B. Matekoni's house near the old Botswana Defence Force Club. She could see that he was in; the green truck which he inevitably drove—in spite of his having a rather better vehicle which he left parked at the garage—stood outside his front door, which he had left half open for the heat. She left the van outside, to save herself from getting in and out to open and shut the gate, and walked up to the house past the few scruffy plants which Mr J.L.B. Matekoni called his garden.

"Ko! Ko!" she called at the door. "Are you there, Mr J.L.B. Matekoni?"

A voice came from the living room. "I am here. I am in, Mma Ramotswe."

Mma Ramotswe walked in, noticing immediately how dusty

and unpolished was the floor of the hall. Ever since Mr J.L.B. Matekoni's sullen and unpleasant maid, Florence, had been sent to prison for harbouring an unlicensed gun, the house had been allowed to get into an unkempt state. She had reminded Mr J.L.B. Matekoni on several occasions to engage a replacement maid, at least until they got married, and he had promised to do so. But he had never acted, and Mma Ramotswe had decided that she would simply have to bring her maid in one day and attempt a spring clean of the whole place.

"Men will live in a very untidy way, if you let them," she had remarked to a friend. "They cannot keep a house or a yard. They don't know how to do it."

She made her way through the hall and into the living room. As she entered, Mr J.L.B. Matekoni, who had been lying full length on his uncomfortable sofa, rose to his feet and tried to make himself look less dishevelled.

"It is good to see you, Mma Ramotswe," he said. "I have not seen you for several days."

"That is true," said Mma Ramotswe. "Perhaps that is because you have been so busy."

"Yes," he said, sitting down again, "I have been very busy. There is so much work to be done."

She said nothing, but watched him as he spoke. There was something wrong; she had been right.

"Are things busy at the garage?" she asked.

He shrugged his shoulders. "Things are always busy at the garage. All the time. People keep bringing their cars in and saying Do this, do that. They think I have ten pairs of hands. That's what they think."

"But do you not expect people to bring their cars to the garage?" she asked gently. "Is that not what a garage is for?"

Mr J.L.B. Matekoni looked at her briefly and then shrugged. "Maybe. But there is still too much work."

Mma Ramotswe glanced about the room, noticing the pile of newspapers on the floor and the small stack of what looked like unopened letters on the table.

"I went to the garage," she said. "I expected to see you there, but they said that you had left early. They said you often left early these days."

Mr J.L.B. Matekoni looked at her, and then transferred his gaze to the floor. "I find it hard to stay there all day, with all that work," he said. "It will get done sooner or later. There are those two boys. They can do it."

Mma Ramotswe gasped. "Those two boys? Those apprentices of yours? But they are the very ones you always said could do nothing. How can you say now that they will do everything that needs to be done? How can you say that?"

Mr J.L.B. Matekoni did not reply.

"Well, Mr J.L.B. Matekoni?" pressed Mma Ramotswe. "What's your answer to that?"

"They'll be all right," he said, in a curious, flat voice. "Let them get on with it."

Mma Ramotswe stood up. There was no point talking to him when he was in this sort of mood—and it certainly was a mood that he seemed to be in. Perhaps he was ill. She had heard that a bout of flu could leave one feeling lethargic for a week or two; perhaps that was the simple explanation of this out-of-character behaviour. In which case, she would just have to wait until he came out of it.

"I've spoken to Mma Makutsi," she said as she prepared to leave. "I think that she can start at the garage sometime in the next few days. I have given her the title of Assistant Manager. I hope that you don't mind."

His reply astonished her.

"Assistant Manager, Manager, Managing Director, Minister of Garages," he said. "Whatever you like. It makes no difference, does it?"

Mma Ramotswe could not think of a suitable reply, so she said goodbye and started to walk out of the door.

"Oh, by the way," said Mr J.L.B. Matekoni as she started to leave the house, "I thought that I might go out to the lands for a little while. I want to see how the planting is going. I might stay out there for a while."

Mma Ramotswe stared at him. "And in the meantime, what happens to the garage?"

Mr J.L.B. Matekoni sighed. "You run it. You and that secretary of yours, the Assistant Manager. Let her do it. It'll be all right."

Mma Ramotswe pursed her lips. "All right," she said. "We'll look after it, Mr J.L.B. Matekoni, until you start to feel better."

"I'm fine," said Mr J.L.B. Matekoni. "Don't worry about me. I'm fine."

SHE DID not drive home to Zebra Drive, although she knew that the two foster children would be waiting there for her. Motholeli, the girl, would have prepared their evening meal by now, and she needed little supervision or help, in spite of her wheelchair. And the boy, Puso, who was inclined to be rather boisterous, would perhaps have expended most of his energy and would be ready for his bath and his bed, both of which Motholeli could prepare for him.

Instead of going home, she turned left at Kudu Road and made her way down past the flats to the house in Odi Way where her friend Dr Moffat lived. Dr Moffat, who used to run the hospital out at Mochudi, had looked after her father and had always been prepared to listen to her when she was in difficulties. She had spoken to him about Note before she had confided in anybody else, and he had told her, as gently as he could, that in his experience such men never changed.

"You must not expect him to become a different man," he had said. "People like that rarely change."

He was a busy man, of course, and she did not wish to intrude on his time, but she decided that she would see if he was in and whether he could throw any light on the way in which Mr J.L.B. Matekoni was behaving. Was there some strange infection doing the rounds which made people all tired and listless? If this were the case, then how long might one expect it to last?

Dr Moffat had just returned home. He welcomed Mma Ramotswe at the door and led her into his study.

"I am worried about Mr J.L.B. Matekoni," she explained. "Let me tell you about him."

He listened for a few minutes and then stopped her.

"I think I know what the trouble might be," he said. "There's a condition called depression. It is an illness like any other illness, and quite common too. It sounds to me as if Mr J.L.B. Matekoni could be depressed."

"And could you treat that?"

"Usually quite easily," said Dr Moffat. "That is, provided that he has depression. If he has, then we have very good antidepressants these days. If all went well, which it probably would, we could have him starting to feel quite a bit better in three weeks or so, maybe even a little bit earlier. These pills take some time to act."

"I will tell him to come and see you straightaway," said Mma Ramotswe.

Dr Moffat looked doubtful. "Sometimes they don't think there's anything wrong with them," he said. "He might not come. It's all very well my telling you what the trouble probably is; he's the one who has to seek treatment."

"Oh, I'll get him to you," said Mma Ramotswe. "You can count on that. I'll make sure that he seeks treatment."

The doctor smiled. "Be careful, Mma Ramotswe," he said. "These things can be difficult."

CHAPTER FIVE

THE GOVERNMENT MAN

THE FOLLOWING morning Mma Ramotswe was at the No. 1 Ladies' Detective Agency before Mma Makutsi arrived. This was unusual, as Mma Makutsi was normally first to arrive and already would have opened the mail and brewed the tea by the time that Mma Ramotswe drove up in her tiny white van. However, this was going to be a difficult day, and she wanted to make a list of the things that she had to do.

"You are very early, Mma," said Mma Makutsi. "Is there anything wrong?"

Mma Ramotswe thought for a moment. In a sense there was a great deal wrong, but she did not want to dishearten Mma Makutsi, and so she put a brave face on it.

"Not really," she said. "But we must start preparing for the move. And also, it will be necessary for you to go and get the garage sorted out. Mr J.L.B. Matekoni is feeling a bit unwell and might be going away for a while. This means that you will not only be Assistant Manager, but Acting Manager. In fact, that is your new title, as from this morning."

Mma Makutsi beamed with pleasure. "I shall do my best as Acting Manager," she said. "I promise that you will not be disappointed."

"Of course I won't be," said Mma Ramotswe. "I know that you are very good at your job."

For the next hour they worked in companionable silence. Mma Ramotswe drafted her list of things to do, then scratched some items out and added others. The early morning was the best time to do anything, particularly in the hot season. In the hot months, before the rains arrived, the temperature soared as the day wore on until the very sky seemed white. In the cool of the morning, when the sun barely warmed the skin and the air was still crisp, any task seemed possible; later, in the full heat of day, both body and mind were sluggish. It was easy to think in the morning—to make lists of things to do—in the afternoon all that one could think about was the end of the day and the prospect of relief from the heat. It was Botswana's one drawback, thought Mma Ramotswe. She knew that it was the perfect country—all Batswana knew that—but it would be even more perfect if the three hottest months could be cooled down.

At nine o'clock Mma Makutsi made a cup of bush tea for Mma Ramotswe and a cup of ordinary tea for herself. Mma Makutsi had tried to accustom herself to bush tea, loyally drinking it for the first few months of her employment, but had eventually confessed that she did not like the taste. From that time on there were two teapots, one for her and one for Mma Ramotswe.

"It's too strong," she said. "And I think it smells of rats."

"It does not," protested Mma Ramotswe. "This tea is for people who really appreciate tea. Ordinary tea is for anyone."

Work stopped while tea was served. This tea break was traditionally a time for catching up on small items of gossip rather than for the broaching of any large subjects. Mma Makutsi enquired after Mr J.L.B. Matekoni, and received a brief report of Mma Ramotswe's unsatisfactory meeting with him.

"He seemed to have no interest in anything," she said. "I could have told him that his house was on fire and he probably wouldn't have bothered very much. It was very strange."

"I have seen people like that before," said Mma Makutsi. "I had a cousin who was sent off to that hospital in Lobatse. I visited her there. There were plenty of people just sitting and staring up at the sky. And there were also people shouting out at the visitors, shouting strange things, all about nothing."

Mma Ramotswe frowned. "That hospital is for mad people," she said. "Mr J.L.B. Matekoni is not going mad."

"Of course not," said Mma Makutsi hurriedly. "He would never go mad. Of course not."

Mma Ramotswe sipped at her tea. "But I still have to get him to a doctor," she said. "I was told that they can treat this sort of behaviour. It is called depression. There are pills which you can take."

"That is good," said Mma Makutsi. "He will get better. I am sure of it."

Mma Ramotswe handed over her mug for refilling. "And what about your family up in Bobonong?" she asked. "Are they well?"

Mma Makutsi poured the rich red tea into the mug. "They are very well, thank you, Mma."

Mma Ramotswe sighed. "I think that it is easier to live in

Bobonong than here in Gaborone. Here we have all these troubles to think about, but in Bobonong there is nothing. Just a whole lot of rocks." She stopped herself. "Of course, it's a very good place, Bobonong. A very nice place."

Mma Makutsi laughed. "You do not have to be polite about Bobonong," she said. "I can laugh about it. It is not a good place for everybody. I would not like to go back, now that I have seen what it is like to live in Gaborone."

"You would be wasted up there," said Mma Ramotswe. "What's the use of a diploma from the Botswana Secretarial College in a place like Bobonong? The ants would eat it."

Mma Makutsi cast an eye up to the wall where her diploma from the Botswana Secretarial College was framed. "We must remember to take that to the new office when we move," she said. "I would not like to leave it behind."

"Of course not," said Mma Ramotswe, who had no diplomas. "That diploma is important for the clients. It gives them confidence."

"Thank you," said Mma Makutsi.

The tea break over, Mma Makutsi went to wash the cups under the standpipe at the back of the building, and it was just as she returned that the client arrived. It was the first client for over a week, and neither of them was prepared for the tall, well-built man who knocked at the door, in the proper Botswana manner, and politely awaited his invitation to enter. Nor were they prepared for the fact that the car which brought him there, complete with smartly attired Government driver, was an official Mercedes-Benz.

* * *

YOU KNOW who I am, Mma?" he said, as he took up the invitation to seat himself in the chair before Mma Ramotswe's desk.

"Of course, I do, Rra," said Mma Ramotswe courteously. "You are something to do with the Government. You are a Government Man. I have seen you in the newspapers many times."

The Government Man made an impatient gesture with his hand. "Yes, there's that, of course. But you know who I am when I am not being a Government Man?"

Mma Makutsi coughed politely, and the Government Man half-turned to face her.

"This is my assistant," explained Mma Ramotswe. "She knows many things."

"You are also the relative of a chief," said Mma Makutsi. "Your father is a cousin of that family. I know that, as I come from that part too."

The Government Man smiled. "That is true."

"And your wife," went on Mma Ramotswe, "she is some relative of the King of Lesotho, is she not? I have seen a photograph of her, too."

The Government Man whistled. "My! My! I can see that I have come to the right place. You people seem to know everything."

Mma Ramotswe nodded to Mma Makutsi and smiled. "It is our business to know things," she said. "A private detective who knows nothing would be no use to anybody. Information is what we deal in. That is our job. Just as your job is giving orders to civil servants."

"I don't just give orders," the Government Man said peevishly. "I have to make policy. I have to make decisions."

"Of course," said Mma Ramotswe hurriedly. "It must be a very big job being a Government Man."

The Government Man nodded. "It is not easy," he said. "And it is not made any easier if one is worried about something. Every night I wake up at two, three and these worries make me sit up in my bed. And then I don't sleep, and when it comes to making decisions in the morning my head is all fuzzy and I cannot think. That is what happens when you are worried."

Mma Ramotswe knew that they were now coming to the reason for the consultation. It was easier to reach it this way, to allow the client to bring the matter up indirectly rather than to launch straight into an enquiry. It seemed less rude, somehow, to allow the matter to be approached in this way.

"We can help with worries," she said. "Sometimes we can make them vanish altogether."

"So I have heard," said the Government Man. "People say that you are a lady who can work miracles. I have heard that."

"You are very kind, Rra." She paused, running over in her mind the various possibilities. It was probably unfaithfulness, which was the most common problem of all the clients who consulted her, particularly if, as in the Government Man's case, they were in busy jobs that took them away from home a great deal. Or it could be something political, which would be new terrain for her. She knew nothing about the workings of political parties, other than that they involved a great deal of intrigue. She had read all about American presidents and the difficulties that they had with this scandal and that scandal, with ladies and burglars and the like. Could there be something like that in Botswana? Surely not, and if there were, she would not choose to get involved. She could not see herself meeting informants on dark corners in the dead of night, or talking in whispers to journalists in bars. On the other hand, Mma Makutsi might appreciate the opportunity . . .

The Government Man raised his hand, as if to command silence. It was an imperious gesture, but then he was the scion of a well-connected family and perhaps these things came naturally.

"I take it that I can speak in complete confidence," he said, glancing briefly at Mma Makutsi.

"My assistant is very confidential," said Mma Ramotswe. "You can trust her."

The Government Man narrowed his eyes. "I hope so," he said. "I know what women are like. They like to talk."

Mma Makutsi's eyes opened wide with indignation.

"I can assure you, Rra," said Mma Ramotswe, her tone steely, "that the No. 1 Ladies' Detective Agency is bound by the strictest principle of confidentiality. The strictest principle. And that goes not only for me but also for that lady over there, Mma Makutsi. If you are in any doubt as to this, then you should find some other detectives. We would not object to that." She paused. "And another thing, Rra. There is a lot of talking that goes on in this country, and most of it, in my opinion, is done by men. The women are usually too busy to talk."

She folded her hands on her desk. She had said it now, and she should not be surprised if the Government Man walked out. A man in his position would not be used to being spoken to in that way and he presumably would not take well to it.

For a moment the Government Man said nothing, but simply stared at Mma Ramotswe.

"So," he said at last. "So. You are quite right. I am sorry that I suggested that you would not be able to keep a secret." Then, turning to Mma Makutsi, he added, "I am sorry that I suggested that thing about you, Mma. It was not a good thing to say."

Mma Ramotswe felt the tension ebb away. "Good," she said. "Now why don't you tell us about these worries? My assistant will boil the kettle. Would you like bush tea or ordinary tea?"

"Bush," said the Government Man. "It's good for worries, I think."

"BECAUSE YOU know who I am," said the Government Man, "I don't have to start at the beginning, or at least at the beginning of the beginning. You know that I am the son of an important man. You know that. And I am the firstborn, which means that I shall be the one to head the family when God calls my father to join him. But I hope that will not be for a long time.

"I have two brothers. One had something wrong with his head and does not talk to anybody. He never talked to anybody and took no interest in anything from the time he was a little boy. So we have sent him out to a cattle post and he is happy there. He stays there all the time and he is no trouble. He just sits and counts the cattle and then, when he has finished, he starts again. That is all that he wants to do in life, even though he is thirty-eight now.

"Then there is my other brother. He is much younger than I am. I am fifty-four, and he is only twenty-six. He is my brother by another mother. My father is old-fashioned and he had two wives and his mother was the younger. There were many girl children—I have nine sisters by various mothers, and many of them have married and have their own children. So we are a big family, but small in the number of important boys, who are really only myself and this brother of twenty-six. He is called Mogadi.

"I am very fond of my brother. Because I am so much older

than he is, I remember him very well from when he was baby. When he grew a bit, I taught him many things. I showed him how to find mopani worms. I showed him how to catch flying ants when they come out of their holes at the first rains. I told him which things you can eat in the bush and which you cannot.

"Then one day he saved my life. We were staying out at the cattle post where our father keeps some of his herds. There were some Basarwa there, because my father's cattle post is not far from the place where these people come in from the Kalahari. It is a very dry place, but there is a windmill which my father set up to pump water for the cattle. There is a lot of water deep underground and it tastes very good. These Basarwa people liked to come and drink this water while they were wandering around and they would do some work for my father in return for some milk from the cows and, if they were lucky, a bit of meat. They liked my father because he never beat them, unlike some people who use sjamboks on them. I have never approved of beating these people, never.

"I took my brother out to see some Basarwa, who were living under a tree not far away. They had some slingshots out of ostrich leather and I wanted to get one for my brother. I took some meat to give to them in exchange. I thought that they might also give us an ostrich egg.

"It was just after the rains, and there was fresh grass and flowers. You know, Mma, what it is like down there when the first rains come. The land is suddenly soft and there are flowers, flowers all around. It is very beautiful, and for a while you forget just how hot and dry and hard it has been. We walked along a path which the animals had made with their hooves, myself in the front and my little brother just behind me. He had a long stick which he was trailing along the ground beside him. I was very happy to be there, with my little brother, and with the fresh grass that I knew would make the cattle fat again.

"He suddenly called out to me, and I stopped. There in the grass beside us was a snake, with its head up off the ground and its mouth open, hissing. It was a big snake, about as long as I am tall, and it had raised about an arm's length of its body off the ground. I knew immediately what sort of snake this was and my heart stopped within me.

"I was very still, because I knew that a movement could make the snake strike and it was only this far from me. It was very close. The snake was looking at me, with those angry eyes that those mambas have, and I thought that it was going to strike me and there was nothing I could do.

"At that moment there was a scraping noise and I saw that my little brother, who was only eleven or twelve at the time, was moving the stick towards the snake, pushing its tip along the ground. The snake moved its head, and before we could make out what was happening, it had struck at the end of the stick. That gave me time to turn round, pick up my brother, and run down the path. The snake disappeared. It had bitten the stick and perhaps it had broken a fang. Whatever happened, it did not choose to follow us.

"He saved my life. You know, Mma, what happens if a person is bitten by a mamba. There is no chance. So from that day I knew that I owed my life to this little brother of mine.

"That was fourteen years ago. Now we do not walk through the bush together very often, but I still love my brother very much and that is why I was unhappy when he came to see me here in Gaborone and told me that he was going to marry a girl he had met when he was a student here at the university. He was doing a BSc there and while he was doing this he came across a girl from Mahalapye. I know her father because he is a clerk in one of the ministries here. I have seen him sitting under the trees with other clerks at lunchtime, and now he waves to me every time he sees my car go past. I waved back at the beginning, but now I cannot be bothered. Why should I wave to this clerk all the time just because his daughter has met my brother?

"My brother is staying down at the farm that we have up north of Pilane. He runs it very well and my father is very content with what he is doing. My father has given him the farm, in fact, and it is now his. This makes him a wealthy man. I have another farm which also belonged to my father, so I am not jealous of that. Mogadi married this girl about three months ago and she moved into the farmhouse that we have. My father and my mother live there. My aunts come and stay for much of the year. It is a very big house and there is room for everybody.

"My mother did not want this woman to marry my brother. She said that she would not make a good wife and that she would only bring unhappiness to the family. I also thought that it was not a good idea, but in my case it was because I thought I knew why she wanted to marry my brother. I did not think that it was because she loved him, or anything like that; I think that she was being encouraged by her father to marry my brother because he came from a rich and important family. I shall never forget, Mma, how her father looked about the place when he came to talk about the marriage with my father. His eyes were wide with greed, and I could see him adding up the value of everything. He even asked my brother how many cattle he had—that from a man who has no cattle himself, I should imagine!

"I accepted my brother's decision, although I thought it was a bad one, and I tried to be as welcoming as possible to this new wife. But it was not easy. This was because all the time I could see that she was plotting to turn my brother against his family. She obviously wants my mother and father out of that house and has made herself very unpleasant to my aunts. It is like a house in which a wasp is trapped, always buzzing away and trying to sting the others.

"That would have been bad enough, I suppose, but then something happened which made me even more concerned. I was down there a few weeks ago and I went to see my brother at the house. When I arrived, I was told that he was not well. I went through to his room and he was lying in bed holding his stomach. He had eaten something very bad, he said; perhaps it was rotten meat.

"I asked him whether he had seen a doctor and he said that it was not serious enough for that. He would get better soon, he thought, even if he felt very ill at that point. I then went and spoke to my mother, who was sitting by herself on the verandah.

"She beckoned me to sit beside her and, having checked to see that there was nobody else about, she told me what was on her mind.

"'That new wife is trying to poison your brother,' she said. 'I saw her go into the kitchen before his meal was served. I saw her. I told him not to finish his meat as I thought it was rotten. If I hadn't told him that, he would have eaten the whole helping and would have died. She's trying to poison him.'

"I asked her why she would do this. 'If she has just married a nice rich husband,' I said, 'why should she want to get rid of him so quickly?'

"My mother laughed. 'Because she'll be much richer as a widow than as a wife,' she said. 'If he dies before she has children, then he has made a will which gives everything to her. The farm, this house, everything. And once she has that, then she can throw us out and all the aunts. But first she has to kill him.'

"I thought at first that this was ridiculous, but the more I pondered it, the more I realised that it provided a very clear motive for this new wife and that it could well be true. I could not talk to my brother about it, as he refuses to hear anything said against his wife, and so I thought that I had better get somebody from outside the family to look into this matter and see what was happening."

Mma Ramotswe raised a hand to interrupt him. "There's the police, Rra. This sounds like something for the police. They are used to dealing with poisoners and people like that. We are not that sort of detective. We help people with the problems in their lives. We are not here to solve crimes."

As Mma Ramotswe spoke, she noticed Mma Makutsi look crestfallen. She knew that her assistant had a different vision of their role; that was the difference, thought Mma Ramotswe between being almost forty and being twenty-eight. At almost forty—or even forty, if one were fussy about dates—one was not on the lookout for excitement; at twenty-eight, if any excitement was to be had, then one wanted to have it. Mma Ramotswe understood, of course. When she had married Note Mokoti, she had yearned for all the glamour that went with being the wife of a well-known musician, a man who turned the heads of all when he entered a room, a man whose very voice seemed redolent of the thrilling notes of jazz that he coaxed out of his shining Selmer trumpet. When the marriage ended, after a pitifully short time, with its only memorial being that minute, sad stone that marked the short life of their premature baby, she had yearned for a life of stability and order. Certainly, excitement was not what she sought, and, indeed Clovis Andersen, author of her professional bible, *The Principles of Private Detection,* had clearly warned, on page two if not on page one itself, that those who became private detectives to find a more exciting life were gravely mistaken as to the nature of the work. *Our job,* he wrote, in a paragraph which had stuck in Mma Ramotswe's mind and which she had quoted in its entirety to Mma Makutsi when she had first engaged her, *is to help people in need to resolve the unresolved questions in their lives. There is very little drama in our calling; rather a process of patient observation, deduction, and analysis. We are sophisticated watchmen, watching and reporting; there is nothing romantic in our job and those who are looking for romance should lay down this manual at this point and do something else.*

Mma Makutsi's eyes had glazed over when Mma Ramotswe had quoted this to her. It was obvious, then, that she thought of the job in a very different way. Now, with no less a person than the Government Man sitting before them talking about family intrigue and possible poisonings, she felt that at last here was an investigation which could allow them to get their teeth into something worthwhile. And, just as this arose, Mma Ramotswe seemed intent on putting off the client!

The Government Man stared at Mma Ramotswe. Her intervention had annoyed him, and it seemed that he was making an effort to control his displeasure. Mma Makutsi noticed that the top of his lip quivered slightly as he listened.

"I cannot go to the police," he said, struggling to keep his voice normal. "What could I say to the police? The police would ask for some proof, even from me. They would say that they could hardly go into that house and arrest a wife who would say that she had done nothing, with the husband there, too, saying *This woman has not done anything. What are you talking about?*"

He stopped and looked at Mma Ramotswe as if he had made out his case.

"Well?" he said abruptly. "If I cannot go to the police, then it becomes the job of a private detective. That's what you people are for, isn't it? Well, Mma?"

Mma Ramotswe returned his gaze, which in itself was a gesture. In traditional society, she should not have looked so hard into the eyes of a man of his rank. That would have been very rude. But times had changed, and she was a citizen of the modern Republic of Botswana, where there was a constitution which guaranteed the dignity of all citizens, lady private detectives among them. That constitution had been upheld from the very day in 1966 when the Union Jack had been taken down in the stadium and that wonderful blue flag had been raised to the ululating of the crowd. It was a record which no other country in Africa, not one, could match. And she was, after all, Precious Ramotswe, daughter of the late Obed Ramotswe, a man whose dignity and worth was the equal of any man, whether he was from a chiefly family or not. He had been able to look into the eye of anyone, right to the day of his death, and she should be able to do so too.

"It is for me to decide whether I take a case, Rra," she said. "I cannot help everybody. I try to help people as much as I can, but if I cannot do a thing, then I say that I am sorry but I cannot help that person. That is how we work in the No. 1 Ladies' Detective Agency. In your case, I just do not see how we could find out what we need to find out. This is a problem inside a family. I do not see how a stranger could find out anything about it."

The Government Man was silent. He glanced at Mma Makutsi, but she dropped her eyes.

"I see," he said after a few moments. "I think you do not want to help me, Mma. Well now, that is very sad for me." He paused. "Do you have a licence for this business, Mma?"

Mma Ramotswe caught her breath. "A licence? Is there a law which requires a licence to be a private detective?"

The Government Man smiled, but his eyes were cold. "Probably not. I haven't checked. But there could be. Regulation, you know. We have to regulate business. That's why we have things like hawkers' licences or general dealers' licences, which we can take away from people who are not suitable to be hawkers or general dealers. You know how that works."

It was Obed Ramotswe who answered; Obed Ramotswe through the lips of his daughter, his Precious.

"I cannot hear what you are saying, Rra. I cannot hear it."

Mma Makutsi suddenly noisily shuffled the papers on her desk.

"Of course, you're right, Mma," she said. "You could not simply go up to that woman and ask her whether she was planning to kill her husband. That would not work."

"No," said Mma Ramotswe. "That is why we cannot do anything here."

"On the other hand," said Mma Makutsi quickly. "I have an idea. I think I know how this might be done."

The Government Man twisted round to face Mma Makutsi. "What is your idea, Mma?"

Mma Makutsi swallowed. Her large glasses seemed to shine with brightness at the force of the idea.

"Well," she began. "It is important to get into the house and listen to what those people are talking about. It is important to watch that woman who is planning to do these wicked things. It is important to look into her heart."

"Yes," said the Government Man. "That is what I want you people to do. You look into that heart and find the evil. Then you shine a torch on the evil and say to my brother: *See! See this bad heart in your wife. See how she is plotting, plotting all the time!*"

"It wouldn't be that simple," said Mma Ramotswe. "Life is not that simple. It just isn't."

"Please, Mma," said the Government Man. "Let us listen to this clever woman in glasses. She has some very good ideas."

Mma Makutsi adjusted her glasses and continued. "There are servants in the house, aren't there?"

"Five," said the Government Man. "Then there are servants for outside. There are men who look after the cattle. And there are the old servants of my father. They cannot work anymore, but they sit in the sun outside the house and my father feeds them well. They are very fat."

"So you see," said Mma Makutsi. "An inside servant sees everything. A maid sees into the bed of the husband and wife, does she not? A cook sees into their stomachs. Servants are always there, watching, watching. They will talk to another servant. Servants know everything."

"So you will go and talk to the servants?" asked the Government Man. "But will they talk to you? They will be worried about their jobs. They will just be quiet and say that there is nothing happening."

"But Mma Ramotswe knows how to talk to people," countered Mma Makutsi. "People talk to her. I have seen it. Can you not get her to stay in your father's house for a few days? Can you not arrange that?"

"Of course I can," said the Government Man. "I can tell my parents that there is a woman who has done me a political favour. She needs to be away from Gaborone for a few days because of some troubles here. They will take her."

Mma Ramotswe glanced at Mma Makutsi. It was not her assistant's place to make suggestions of this sort, particularly when their effect would be to railroad her into taking a case which she did not wish to take. She would have to speak to Mma Makutsi about this, but she did not wish to embarrass her in front of this man with his autocratic ways and his pride. She would accept the case, not because his thinly veiled threat had worked—that she had clearly stood up to by saying that she could not hear him—but because she had been presented with a way of finding out what needed to be found out.

"Very well," she said. "We will take this on, Rra. Not because of anything you have said to me, particularly those things that I did not hear." She paused, allowing the effect of her words to be felt. "But I will decide what to do once I am there. You must not interfere."

The Government Man nodded enthusiastically. "That is fine, Mma. I am very happy with that. And I am sorry that I said things which I should not have said. You must know that my brother is very important to me. I would not have said anything if it had not been for my fears for my brother. That is all."

Mma Ramotswe looked at him. He did love his brother. It could not be easy to see him married to a woman whom he mistrusted so strongly. "I have already forgotten what was said, Rra," she said. "You need not worry."

The Government Man rose to his feet. "Will you start tomorrow?" he said. "I shall make the arrangements."

"No," said Mma Ramotswe. "I will start in a few days' time. I have much to do here in Gaborone. But do not worry, if there is anything that can be done for your poor brother, I shall do it. Once we take on a case, we do not treat it lightly. I promise you that."

The Government Man reached across the desk and took her hand in his. "You are a very kind woman, Mma. What they say about you is true. Every word."

He turned to Mma Makutsi. "And you, Mma. You are a clever lady. If you ever decide that you are tired of being a private detective, come and work for the Government. The Government needs women like you. Most of the women we have working in Government are no good. They sit and paint their nails. I have seen them. You would work hard, I think."

Mma Ramotswe was about to say something, but the Government Man was already on his way out. From the window, they saw his driver open the car door smartly and slam it shut behind him.

"If I did go to work for the Government," said Mma Makutsi, adding quickly, "and I'm not going to do that, of course. But I wonder how long it would be before I had a car like that, and a driver."

Mma Ramotswe laughed. "Don't believe everything he says," she said. "Men like that can make all sorts of promises. And he is a very stupid man. Very proud too."

"But he was telling the truth about the brother's wife?" asked Mma Makutsi anxiously.

"Probably," said Mma Ramotswe. "I don't think he made that up. But remember what Clovis Andersen says. Every story has two sides. So far, we've only heard one. The stupid side."

LIFE WAS becoming complicated, thought Mma Ramotswe. She had just agreed to take on a case which could prove far from simple, and which would take her away from Gaborone. That in itself was problematic enough, but the whole situation became much more difficult when one thought about Mr J.L.B. Matekoni and Tlokweng Road Speedy Motors. And then there was the question of the children; now that they had settled into her house at Zebra Drive she would have to establish some sort of routine for them. Rose, her maid, was a great help in that respect, but she could not shoulder the whole burden herself.

The list she had begun to compose earlier that morning had been headed by the task of preparing the office for a move. Now she thought that she should promote the issue of the garage to the top of the list and put the office second. Then she could fit the children in below that: she wrote SCHOOL in capital letters and a telephone number beneath that. This was followed by GET MAN TO FIX FRIDGE. TAKE ROSE'S SON TO THE DOCTOR FOR HIS ASTHMA, and finally she wrote: DO SOMETHING ABOUT BAD WIFE.

"Mma Makutsi," she said. "I think that I am going to take

you over to the garage. We cannot let Mr J.L.B. Matekoni down, even if he is behaving strangely. You must start your duties as Acting Manager right now. I will take you in the van."

Mma Makutsi nodded. "I am ready, Mma," she said. "I am ready to manage."

CHAPTER SIX

UNDER NEW MANAGEMENT

TLOKWENG ROAD Speedy Motors stood a short distance off the road, half a mile beyond the two big stores that had been built at the edge of the district known as the Village. It was in a cluster of three buildings: a general dealer's shop that stocked everything from cheap clothing to paraffin and golden syrup, and a builder's yard which dealt in timber and sheets of corrugated iron for roofs. The garage was at the eastern end, with several thorn trees around it and an old petrol pump to the front. Mr J.L.B. Matekoni had been promised a more modern pump, but the petrol company was not keen for him to sell petrol in competition with their more modern outlets and they conveniently forgot this promise. They continued to deliver petrol, as they were contractually bound to do, but they did it without enthusiasm and tended to forget when they had agreed to come. As a result, the fuel storage tanks were frequently empty.

None of that mattered very much. Clients came to Tlokweng Road Speedy Motors because they wanted their cars to be fixed by Mr J.L.B. Matekoni rather than to buy petrol. They were people who understood the difference between a good mechanic and one who merely fixed cars. A good mechanic understood cars; he could diagnose a problem just by listening to an engine running, in much the same way as an experienced doctor may see what is wrong just by looking at the patient.

"Engines talk to you," he explained to his apprentices. "Listen to them. They are telling you what is wrong with them, if only you listen."

Of course, the apprentices did not understand what he meant. They had an entirely different view of machinery and were quite incapable of appreciating that engines might have moods, and emotions, that an engine might feel stressed or under pressure, or relieved and at ease. The presence of the apprentices was an act of charity on the part of Mr J.L.B. Matekoni, who was concerned that there should be enough properly trained mechanics in Botswana to replace his generation when it eventually retired.

"Africa will get nowhere until we have mechanics," he once remarked to Mma Ramotswe. "Mechanics are the first stone in the building. Then there are other people on top. Doctors. Nurses. Teachers. But the whole thing is built on mechanics. That is why it is important to teach young people to be mechanics."

Now, driving up to Tlokweng Road Speedy Motors, Mma Ramotswe and Mma Makutsi saw one of the apprentices at the wheel of a car while the other was pushing it slowly forward into the workshop. As they approached, the apprentice who was doing the pushing abandoned his task to look at them and the car rolled backwards.

Mma Ramotswe parked her tiny white van under a tree and she and Mma Makutsi walked over to the office entrance.

"Good morning, Bomma," the taller of the two apprentices said. "Your suspension on that van of yours is very bad. You are too heavy for it. See how it goes down on one side. We can fix it for you."

"There is nothing wrong with it," retorted Mma Ramotswe. "Mr J.L.B. Matekoni himself looks after that van. He has never said anything about suspension."

"But he is saying nothing about anything these days," said the apprentice. "He is quite silent."

Mma Makutsi stopped and looked at the boy. "I am Mma Makutsi," she said, staring at him through her large glasses. "I am the Acting Manager. If you want to talk about suspension, then you can come and talk to me in the office. In the meantime, what are you doing? Whose car is that and what are you doing to it?"

The apprentice looked over his shoulder for support from his friend.

"It is the car of that woman who lives behind the police station. I think she is some sort of easy lady." He laughed. "She uses this car to pick up men and now it will not start. So she can get no men. Ha!"

Mma Makutsi bristled with anger. "It would not start, would it?"

"Yes," said the apprentice. "It would not start. And so Charlie and I had to drive over with the truck and tow it in. Now we are pushing it into the garage to look at the engine. It will be a big job, I think. Maybe a new starter motor. You know these things. They cost a lot of money and it is good that the men give that woman all that money so she can pay. Ha!"

Mma Makutsi moved her glasses down on her nose and stared at the boy over the top of them.

"And what about the battery?" she said. "Maybe it's the battery. Did you try to jump-start it?"

The apprentice stopped smiling.

"Well?" asked Mma Ramotswe. "Did you take the leads? Did you try?"

The apprentice shook his head. "It is an old car. There will be something else wrong with it."

"Nonsense," said Mma Makutsi. "Open the front. Have you got a good battery in the workshop? Put the leads on that and try."

The apprentice looked at the other, who shrugged.

"Come on," said Mma Makutsi. "I have a lot to do in the office. Get going please."

Mma Ramotswe said nothing, but watched with Mma Makutsi as the apprentices moved the car the last few yards into the workshop and then linked the battery leads to a fresh battery. Then, sullenly, one of them climbed into the driver's seat and tried the ignition. The engine started immediately.

"Charge it up," said Mma Makutsi. "Then change the oil for that woman and take the car back to her. Tell her that you are sorry it has taken longer than necessary to fix, but that we have given her an oil change for nothing to make up for it." She turned to Mma Ramotswe, who was standing smiling beside her. "Customer loyalty is very important. If you do something for the customer, then the customer is going to stay with you forever. That is very important in business."

"Very," agreed Mma Ramotswe. She had harboured doubts about Mma Makutsi's ability to manage the garage, but these were well on their way to being allayed.

"Do you know much about cars?" she asked her assistant casually, as they began to sort out the crowded surface of Mr J.L.B. Matekoni's desk.

"Not very much," answered Mma Makutsi. "But I am good with typewriters, and one machine is very much like another, don't you think?"

THEIR IMMEDIATE task was to find out what cars were waiting to be attended to and which were booked in for future attention. The elder of the two apprentices, Charlie, was summoned into the office and asked to give a list of outstanding work. There were eight cars, it transpired, which were parked at the back of the garage waiting for parts. Some of these had been ordered and others had not. Once a list had been made, Mma Makutsi telephoned each supplier in turn and enquired about the part.

"Mr J.L.B. Matekoni is very cross," she said sharply. "And we will not be able to pay you for past orders if you do not let us get on with new work. Do you understand that?"

Promises were made, and, for the most part, kept. Parts began to arrive several hours later, brought round by the suppliers themselves. These were duly labelled—something which had not happened before, said the apprentices—and placed on a bench, in order of urgency. In the meantime, their work coordinated by Mma Makutsi, the apprentices busily fitted parts, tested engines, and eventually handed over each vehicle to Mma Makutsi for testing. She interrogated them as to what had been done, sometimes asking to inspect the work itself, and then, being unable to drive, she handed the vehicle over to Mma Ramotswe for a test run before she telephoned the owner to tell them that the work was finished. Only half the bill would be charged, she explained, to compensate for the length of the delay. This mollified every owner, except one, who announced that he would be going elsewhere in future.

"Then you will not be able to take advantage of our free service offer," said Mma Makutsi quietly. "That is a pity."

This brought the necessary change of mind, and at the end of the day Tlokweng Road Speedy Motors had returned six cars to their owners, all of whom had appeared to have forgiven them.

"It has been a good first day," said Mma Makutsi, as she and Mma Ramotswe watched the exhausted apprentices walking off down the road. "Those boys worked very hard and I have rewarded them with a bonus of fifty pula each. They are very happy and I'm sure that they will become better apprentices. You'll see."

Mma Ramotswe was bemused. "I think you may be right, Mma," she said. "You are an exceptional manager."

"Thank you," said Mma Makutsi. "But we must go home now, as we have a lot to do tomorrow."

Mma Ramotswe drove her assistant home in the tiny white van, along the roads that were crowded with people returning from work. There were minibuses, overloaded and listing alarmingly to one side with their burden, bicycles with passengers perched on the carriers, and people simply walking, arms swinging, whistling, thinking, hoping. She knew the road well, having driven Mma Makutsi home on many occasions, and was familiar with the ramshackle houses with their knots of staring, inquisitive children who seemed to populate such areas. She dropped her assistant at her front gate and watched her walk round to the back of the building and the breeze-block shack in which she lived. She thought she saw a figure in the doorway, a shadow perhaps, but then Mma Makutsi turned round and Mma Ramotswe, who could not be seen to be watching her, had to drive off.

CHAPTER SEVEN

THE GIRL WITH THREE LIVES

NOT EVERYBODY had a maid, of course, but if you were in a well-paid job and had a house of the size which Mma Ramotswe did, then not to employ a maid—or indeed not to support several domestic servants—would have been seen as selfishness. Mma Ramotswe knew that there were countries where people had no servants, even when they were well enough off to do so. She found this inexplicable. If people who were in a position to have servants chose not to do so, then what were the servants to do?

In Botswana, every house in Zebra Drive—or indeed every house with over two bedrooms—would be likely to have a servant. There were laws about how much domestic servants should be paid, but these were often flouted. There were people who treated their servants very badly, who paid them very little and expected them to work all hours of the day, and these people, as far as Mma Ramotswe knew, were probably in the majority. This was Botswana's dark secret—this exploitation—which nobody liked to talk about. Certainly nobody liked to talk about how the Masarwa had been treated in the past, as slaves effectively, and if one mentioned it, people looked shifty and changed the subject. But it had happened, and it was still happening here and there for all that anybody knew. Of course, this sort of thing happened throughout Africa. Slavery had been a great wrong perpetrated against Africa, but there had always been willing African slavers, who sold their own people, and there were still vast legions of Africans working for a pittance in conditions of near-slavery. These people were quiet people, weak people, and the domestic servants were amongst them.

Mma Ramotswe was astonished that people could behave so callously to their servants. She herself had been in the house of a friend who had referred, quite casually, to the fact that her maid was given five days holiday a year, and unpaid at that. This friend boasted that she had managed to cut the maid's wages recently because she thought her lazy.

"But why doesn't she go, if you do such a thing?" asked Mma Ramotswe.

The friend had laughed. "Go where? There are plenty of people wanting her job, and she knows it. She knows that I could get somebody to do her job for half the wages she's getting."

Mma Ramotswe had said nothing, but had mentally ended the friendship at that point. This had given her cause for thought. Can one be the friend of a person who behaves badly? Or is the case that bad people can only have bad friends, because only other bad people will have sufficient in common with them to be friends? Mma Ramotswe thought of notoriously bad people. There was Idi Amin, for example, or Henrik Verwoerd. Idi Amin, of course, had something wrong with him; perhaps he was not bad in the same way as Mr Verwoerd, who had seemed quite sane, but who had a heart of ice. Had anybody loved Mr Verwoerd? Had anybody held his hand? Mma Ramotswe assumed that they had; there had been people at his funeral, had there not, and did they not weep, just as people weep at the funerals of good men? Mr Verwoerd had his people, and perhaps not all of his people were bad. Now that things had changed over the border in South Africa, these people still had to go on living. Perhaps they now understood the wrong they had done; even if they did not, they had been forgiven, for the most part. The ordinary people of Africa tended not to have room in their hearts for hatred. They were sometimes foolish, like people anywhere, but they did not bear grudges, as Mr Mandela had shown the world. As had Seretse Khama, thought Mma Ramotswe; though nobody outside Botswana seemed to remember him anymore. Yet he was one of Africa's great men, and had shaken the hand of her father, Obed Ramotswe, when he had visited Mochudi to talk to the people. And she, Precious Ramotswe, then a young girl, had seen him step out of his car and the people had flocked about him and among them, holding his old battered hat in his hand, was her father. And as the Khama had taken her father's hand, her own heart had swelled with pride; and she remembered the occasion every time she looked at the photograph of the great statesman on her mantelpiece.

Her friend who treated her maid badly was not a wicked person. She behaved well towards her family and she had always been kind to Mma Ramotswe, but when it came to her maid—and Mma Ramotswe had met this maid, who seemed an agreeable, hardworking woman from Molepolole—she seemed to have little concern for her feelings. It occurred to Mma Ramotswe that such behaviour was no more than ignorance; an inability to understand the hopes and aspirations of others. That understanding, thought Mma Ramotswe, was the beginning of all morality. If you knew how a person was feeling, if you could imagine yourself in her position, then surely it would be impossible to inflict further pain. Inflicting pain in such circumstances would be like hurting oneself.

Mma Ramotswe knew that there was a great deal of debate about morality, but in her view it was quite simple. In the first place, there was the old Botswana morality, which was simply right. If a person stuck to this, then he would be doing the right thing and need not worry about it. There were other moralities, of course; there were the Ten Commandments, which she had learned by heart at Sunday School in Mochudi all those years ago; these were also right in the same, absolute way. These codes of morality were like the Botswana Penal Code; they had to be obeyed to the letter. It was no good pretending you were the High Court of Botswana and deciding which parts you were going to observe and which you were not. Moral codes were not designed to be selective, nor indeed were they designed to be questioned. You could not say that you would observe this prohibition but not that. *I shall not commit theft—certainly not—but adultery is another matter: wrong for other people, but not for me.*

Most morality, thought Mma Ramotswe, was about doing the right thing because it had been identified as such by a long process of acceptance and observance. You simply could not create your own morality because your experience would never be enough to do so. What gives you the right to say that you know better than your ancestors? Morality is for everybody, and this means that the views of more than one person are needed to create it. That was what made the modern morality, with its emphasis on individuals and the working out of an individual position, so weak. If you gave people the chance to work out their morality, then they would work out the version which was easiest for them and which allowed them to do what suited them for as much of the time as possible. That, in Mma Ramotswe's view, was simple selfishness, whatever grand name one gave to it.

Mma Ramotswe had listened to a World Service broadcast on her radio one day which had simply taken her breath away. It was about philosophers who called themselves existentialists and who, as far as Mma Ramotswe could ascertain, lived in France. These French people said that you should live in a way which made you feel real, and that the real thing to do was the right thing too. Mma Ramotswe had listened in astonishment. You did not have to go to France to meet existentialists, she reflected; there were many existentialists right here in Botswana. Note Mokoti, for example. She had been married to an existentialist herself, without even knowing it. Note, that selfish man who never once put himself out for another—not even for his wife—would have approved of existentialists, and they of him. It was very existentialist, perhaps, to go out to bars every night while your pregnant wife stayed at home, and even more existentialist to go off with girls—young existentialist girls—you met in bars. It was a good life being an existentialist, although not too good for all the other, nonexistentialist people around one.

* * *

MMA RAMOTSWE did not treat her maid, Rose, in an existentialist way. Rose had worked for her from the day that she first moved in to Zebra Drive. There was a network of unemployed people, Mma Ramotswe discovered, and this sent out word of anybody who was moving into a new house and who might be expected to need a servant. Rose had arrived at the house within an hour of Mma Ramotswe herself.

"You will need a maid, Mma," she had said. "And I am a very good maid. I will work very hard and will not be a trouble to you for the rest of your life. I am ready to start now."

Mma Ramotswe had made an immediate judgement. She saw before her a respectable-looking woman, neatly presented, of about thirty. But she saw, too, a mother, one of whose children was waiting by the gate, staring at her. And she wondered what the mother had said to her child. *We shall eat tonight if this woman takes me as her maid. Let us hope. You wait here and stand on your toe.* Stand on your toe. That is what one said in Setswana if one hoped that something would happen. It was the same as the expression which white people used: cross your fingers.

Mma Ramotswe glanced towards the gate and saw that the child was indeed standing on her toe, and she knew then that there was only one answer she could give.

She looked at the woman. "Yes," she said. "I need a maid, and I will give the job to you, Mma."

The woman clapped her hands together in gratitude and waved to the child. I am lucky, thought Mma Ramotswe. I am lucky that I can make somebody so happy just by saying something.

Rose moved in immediately and rapidly proved her worth. Zebra Drive had been left in a bad way by its previous owners, who had been untidy people, and there was dust in every corner. Over three days she swept and polished, until the house smelled of floor wax and every surface shone. Not only that, but she was an expert cook and a magnificent ironer. Mma Ramotswe was well dressed, but she always found it difficult to find the energy to iron her blouses as much as she might have wished. Rose did this with a passion that was soon reflected in starched seams and expanses to which creases were quite alien.

Rose took up residence in the servants' quarters in the back yard. This consisted of a small block of two rooms, with a shower and toilet to one side and a covered porch under which a cooking fire might be made. She slept in one of the rooms, while her two small children slept in the other. There were other, older children, including one who was a carpenter and earning a good wage. But even with that, the expenses of living were such as to leave very little over, particularly since her younger son had asthma and needed expensive inhalers to help him breathe.

NOW, COMING home after dropping off Mma Makutsi, Mma Ramotswe found Rose in the kitchen, scouring a blackened cooking pot. She enquired politely after the maid's day and was told that it had been a very good one.

"I have helped Motholeli with her bath," she said. "And now she is through there, reading to her little brother. He has been running round all day and is tired, tired. He will be asleep very soon. Only the thought of his supper is keeping him awake, I think."

Mma Ramotswe thanked her and smiled. It had been a

month since the children had arrived from the orphanage, by way of Mr J.L.B. Matekoni, and she was still getting used to their presence in the house. They had been his idea—and indeed he had not consulted her before he had agreed to act as their foster father—but she had accepted the situation and had quickly taken to them. Motholeli, who was in a wheelchair, had proved herself useful about the house and had expressed an interest in mending cars—much to Mr J.L.B. Matekoni's delight. Her brother, who was much younger, was more difficult to fathom. He was active enough, and spoke politely when spoken to, but seemed to be keener on his own company, or that of his sister, than on that of other children. Motholeli had made some friends already, but the boy seemed shy of doing so.

She had started at Gaborone Secondary School, which was not far away, and was happy there. Each morning, one of the other girls from her class would arrive at the door and volunteer to push the wheelchair to school.

Mma Ramotswe had been impressed.

"Do the teachers tell you to do this?" she asked one of them.

"They do not, Mma," came the reply. "We are the friends of this girl. That is why we do this."

"You are kind girls," said Mma Ramotswe. "You will be kind ladies in due course. Well done."

The boy had been found a place at the local primary school, but Mma Ramotswe hoped that Mr J.L.B. Matekoni would pay to send him to Thornhill. This cost a great deal of money, and now she wondered whether it would ever be possible. That was just one of the many things which would have to be sorted out. There was the garage, the apprentices, the house near the old Botswana Defence Force Club, and the children. There was also the wedding—whenever that would be—although Mma Ramotswe hardly dared think of that at present.

She went through to the living room, to see the boy seated beside his sister's wheelchair, listening to her as she read.

"So," said Mma Ramotswe. "You are reading a story to your little brother. Is it a good one?"

Motholeli looked round and smiled.

"It is not a story, Mma," she said. "Or rather, it is not a proper story from a book. It is a story I have written at school, and I am reading it to him."

Mma Ramotswe joined them, perching on the arm of the sofa.

"Why don't you start off again?" she said. "I would like to hear your story."

MY NAME is Motholeli and I am thirteen years old, almost fourteen. I have a brother, who is seven. My mother and father are late. I am very sad about this, but I am happy that I am not late too and that I have my brother.

I am a girl who has had three lives. My first life was when I lived with my mother and my aunts and uncles, up in the Makadikadi, near Nata. That was long ago, and I was very small. They were bush people and they moved from place to place. They knew how to find food in the bush by digging for roots. They were very clever people, but nobody liked them.

My mother gave me a bracelet made out of ostrich skin, with pieces of ostrich eggshell stitched into it. I still have that. It is the only thing I have from my mother, now that she is late.

After she died, I rescued my little brother, who had been buried in the sand with her. He was just under the sand, and so I scraped it off his face and saw that he was still breathing. I remember picking him up and running through the bush until I found a road. A man came down the road in a truck and when he saw me he stopped and took me to Francistown. I do not remember what happened there, but I was given to a woman who said that I could live in her yard. They had a small shed, which was very hot when the sun was on it, but which was cool at night. I slept there with my baby brother.

I fed him with the food that I was given from that house. I used to do things for those kind people. I did their washing and hung it out on the line. I cleaned some pots for them too, as they did not have a servant. There was a dog who lived in the yard too, and it bit me one day, sharply, in my foot. The woman's husband was very cross with the dog after that and he beat it with a wooden pole. That dog is late now, after all that beating for being wicked.

I became very sick, and the woman took me to the hospital. They put needles into me and they took out some of my blood. But they could not make me better, and after a while I could not walk anymore. They gave me crutches, but I was not very good at walking with them. Then they found a wheelchair; which meant that I could go home again. But the woman said that she could not have a wheelchair girl living in her yard, as that would not look good and people would say: *What are you doing having a girl in a wheelchair in your yard? That is very cruel.*

Then a man came by who said that he was looking for orphans to take to his orphan farm. There was a lady from the Government with him who told me that I was very lucky to get a place on such a fine orphan farm. I could take my brother, and we would be very happy living there. But I must always remember to love Jesus, this woman said. I replied that I was ready to love Jesus and that I would make my little brother love him too.

That was the end of my first life. My second life started on the day that I arrived at the orphan farm. We had come down from Francistown in a truck, and I was very hot and uncomfortable in the back. I could not get out, as the truck driver did not know what to do with a girl in a wheelchair. So when I arrived at the orphan farm, my dress was wet and I was very ashamed, especially since all the other orphans were standing there watching us come to their place. One of the ladies there told the other children to go off and play, and not to stare at us, but they only went a little way and they watched me from behind the trees.

All the orphans lived in houses. Each house had about ten orphans in it and had a mother who looked after them. My housemother was a kind lady. She gave me new clothes and a cupboard to keep my things in. I had never had a cupboard before and I was very proud of it. I was also given some special clips which I could put in my hair. I had never had such beautiful things, and I would keep them under my pillow, where they were safe. Sometimes at night I would wake up and think how lucky I was. But I would also cry sometimes, because I was thinking of my first life and I would be thinking about my uncles and aunts and wondering where they were now. I could see the stars from my bed, through a gap in the curtain, and I thought: if they looked up, they would see the same stars, and we would be looking at them at the same time. But I wondered if they remembered me, because I was just a girl and I had run away from them.

I was very happy at the orphan farm. I worked hard, and Mma Potokwane, who was the matron, said that one day, if I was lucky, she would find somebody who would be new parents for us. I did not think that this was possible, as nobody would want to take a girl in a wheelchair when there were plenty of first-class orphan girls who could walk very well and who would be looking for a home too.

But she was right. I did not think that it would be Mr J.L.B. Matekoni who took us, but I was very pleased when he said that we could go to live in his house. That is how my third life began.

They made us a special cake when we left the orphan farm, and we ate it with the housemother. She said that she always felt very sad when one of the orphans went, as it was like a member of the family leaving. But she knew Mr J.L.B. Matekoni very well, and she told me that he was one of the best men in Botswana. I would be very happy in his house, she said.

So I went to his house, with my small brother, and we soon met his friend, Mma Ramotswe, who is going to be married to Mr J.L.B. Matekoni. She said that she would be my new mother, and she brought us to her house, which is better for children than Mr J.L.B. Matekoni's house. I have a very good bedroom there, and I have been given many clothes. I am very happy that there are people like this in Botswana. I have had a very fortunate life and I thank Mma Ramotswe and Mr J.L.B. Matekoni from my heart.

I would like to be a mechanic when I grow up. I shall help Mr J.L.B. Matekoni in his garage and at night I will mend Mma Ramotswe's clothes and cook her meals. Then, when they are very old, they will be able to be proud of me and say that I have been a good daughter for them and a good citizen of Botswana.

That is the story of my life. I am an ordinary girl from Botswana, but it is very lucky to have three lives. Most people only have one life.

This story is true. I have not made any of it up. It is all true.

AFTER THE girl had finished, they were all silent. The boy looked up at his sister and smiled. He thought: I am a lucky boy to have such a clever sister. I hope that God will give her back her legs one day. Mma Ramotswe looked at the girl and laid a hand gently on her shoulder. She thought: I will look after this child. I am now her mother. Rose, who had been listening from the corridor, looked down at her shoes and thought: What a strange way of putting it: three lives.

CHAPTER EIGHT

LOW SEROTONIN LEVELS

THE FIRST thing that Mma Ramotswe did the following morning was to telephone Mr J.L.B. Matekoni in his house near the old Botswana Defence Force Club. They often telephoned one another early in the morning—at least since they had become engaged—but it was usually Mr J.L.B. Matekoni who called. He would wait until the time Mma Ramotswe would have had her cup of bush tea, which she liked to drink out in the garden, before he would dial her number and declare himself formally, as he always liked to do: "This is Mr J.L.B. Matekoni, Mma. Have you slept well?"

The telephone rang for over a minute before it was picked up.

"Mr J.L.B. Matekoni? This is me. How are you? Have you slept well?"

The voice at the other end of the line sounded confused, and Mma Ramotswe realised that she had woken him up.

"Oh. Yes. Oh. I am awake now. It is me."

Mma Ramotswe persisted with the formal greeting. It was important to ask a person if he had slept well; an old tradition, but one which had to be maintained.

"But have you slept well, Rra?"

Mr J.L.B. Matekoni's voice was flat when he replied. "I do not think so. I spent all night thinking and there was no sleep. I only went to sleep when everybody else was waking up. I am very tired now."

"That is a pity, Rra. I'm sorry that I woke you up. You must go back to bed and get some sleep. You cannot live without sleep."

"I know that," said Mr J.L.B. Matekoni irritably. "I am always trying to sleep these days, but I do not succeed. It is as if there is some strange animal in my room which does not want me to sleep and keeps nudging me."

"Animal?" asked Mma Ramotswe. "What is this animal?"

"There is no animal. Or at least there is no animal when I turn on the light. It's just that I think there is one there who does not want me to sleep. That is all I said. There is really no animal."

Mma Ramotswe was silent. Then she asked, "Are you feeling well, Rra? Maybe you are ill."

Mr J.L.B. Matekoni snorted. "I am not ill. My heart is thumping away inside me. My lungs are filling up with air. I am just fed up with all the problems that there are. I am worried that they will find out about me. Then everything will be over."

Mma Ramotswe frowned. "Find out about you? Who will find out about what?"

Mr J.L.B. Matekoni dropped his voice. "You know what I'm talking about. You know very well."

"I know nothing, Rra. All I know is that you are saying some very strange things."

"Ha! You say that, Mma, but you know very well what I am talking about. I have done very wicked things in my life and now they are going to find out about me and arrest me. I will be punished, and you will be very ashamed of me, Mma. I can tell you that."

Mma Ramotswe's voice was small now as she struggled to come to terms with what she had heard. Could it be true that Mr J.L.B. Matekoni had committed some terrible crime which he had concealed from her? And had he now been found out? It seemed impossible that this could be true; he was a fine man, incapable of doing anything dishonourable, but then such people sometimes had a murky secret in their past. Everybody has done at least one thing to be ashamed of, or so she had heard. Bishop Makhulu himself had given a talk about this once to the Women's Club and he had said that he had never met anybody, even in the Church, who had not done something which he or she later regretted. Even the saints had done something bad; St Francis, perhaps, had stamped on a pigeon—no, surely not—but perhaps he had done something else which caused him regret. For her own part, there were many things which she would rather she had not done, starting from the time that she had put treacle on the best dress of another girl when she was six because she did not have such a dress herself. She still saw that person from time to time—she lived in Gaborone and was married to a man who worked at the diamond-sorting building. Mma Ramotswe wondered whether she should confess, even over thirty years later, and tell this woman what she had done, but she could not bring herself to do so. But every time that this woman greeted her in a friendly manner, Mma Ramotswe remembered how she had taken the tin of treacle and poured it over the pink material when the girl had left the dress in their classroom one day. She would have to tell her one day; or perhaps she could ask Bishop Makhulu to write a letter on her behalf. *One of my flock seeks your forgiveness, Mma. She is grievously burdened with a wrong which she committed against you many years ago. Do you remember your favourite pink dress . . .*

If Mr J.L.B. Matekoni had done something like that—perhaps poured engine oil over somebody—then he should not worry about it. There were few wrongs, short of murder, which could not be put right again. Many of them, indeed, were more minor than the transgressor imagined, and could be safely left where they lay in the past. And even the more serious ones might be forgiven once they were acknowledged. She should reassure Mr J.L.B. Matekoni; it was easy to inflate some tiny matter if one spent the night worrying about it.

"We have all done something wrong in our lives, Rra," she said. "You, me, Mma Makutsi, the Pope even. None of us can say that we have been perfect. That is not how people are. You must not worry about it. Just tell me what it was. I'm sure that I'll be able to set your mind at rest."

"Oh, I cannot do that, Mma. I cannot even start to tell you. You would be very shocked. You would never want to see me again. You see, I am not worthy of you. You are too good for me, Mma."

Mma Ramotswe felt herself becoming exasperated. "You are not talking sense. Of course you are worthy of me. I am just an ordinary person. You are a perfectly good man. You are good at your job and people think a great deal of you. Where does the British High Commissioner take his car to be serviced? To you. Where does the orphan farm turn when it needs somebody to fix something? To you. You have a very good garage and I am honoured that I am going to marry you. That is all there is to it."

Her remarks were greeted with silence. Then: "But you do not know how bad I am. I have never told you of these wicked things."

"Then tell me. Tell me now. I am strong."

"Oh I cannot do that, Mma. You would be shocked."

Mma Ramotswe realised that the conversation was getting nowhere, and so she changed her tack.

"And speaking of your garage," she said. "You were not there yesterday, or the day before. Mma Makutsi is running it for you. But that cannot go on forever."

"I am pleased that she is running it," said Mr J.L.B. Matekoni flatly. "I am not feeling very strong at the moment. I think that I should stay here in my house. She will look after everything. Please thank her for me."

Mma Ramotswe took a deep breath. "You are not well, Mr J.L.B. Matekoni. I think that I can arrange for you to see a doctor. I have spoken to Dr Moffat. He says that he will see you. He thinks it is a good idea."

"I am not broken," said Mr J.L.B. Matekoni. "I do not need to see Dr Moffat. What can he do for me? Nothing."

IT HAD not been a reassuring call, and Mma Ramotswe spent an anxious few minutes pacing about her kitchen after she had rung off. It was clear to her that Dr Moffat had been right;

that Mr J.L.B. Matekoni was suffering from an illness—depression, he had called it—but now she was more worried about the terrible thing that he said he had done. There was no less likely murderer than Mr J.L.B. Matekoni, but what if it transpired that this was what he was? Would it change her feelings for him if she discovered that he had killed somebody, or would she tell herself that it was not really his fault, that he was defending himself when he hit his victim over the head with a spanner? This is what the wives and girlfriends of murderers inevitably did. They never accepted that their man could be capable of being a murderer. Mothers were like that, too. The mothers of murderers always insisted that their sons were not as bad as people said. Of course, for a mother, the man remained a small boy, no matter how old he became, and small boys can never be guilty of murder.

Of course, Note Mokoti could have been a murderer. He was quite capable of killing a man in cold blood, because he had no feelings. It was easy to imagine Note stabbing somebody and walking away as casually as if he had done no more than shake his victim's hand. When he had beaten her, as he had on so many occasions before he left, he had shown no emotion. Once, when he had split the skin above her eyebrow with a particularly savage blow, he had stopped to examine his handiwork as if he were a doctor examining a wound.

"You will need to take that to the hospital," he had said, his voice quite even. "That is a bad cut. You must be more careful."

The one thing that she was grateful for in the whole Note episode was that her Daddy was still alive when she left him. At least he had the pleasure of knowing that his daughter was no longer with that man, even if he had had almost two years of suffering while she was with him. When she had gone to him and told him that Note had left, he had said nothing about her foolishness in marrying him, even if he might have thought about it. He simply said that she must come back to his house, that he would always look after her, and that he hoped that her life would be better now. He had shown such dignity, as he always did. And she had wept, and gone to him and he had told her that she was safe with him and that she need not fear that man again.

But Note Mokoti and Mr J.L.B. Matekoni were totally different men. Note was the one who had committed the crimes, not Mr J.L.B. Matekoni. And yet, why did he insist that he had done something terrible if he had not? Mma Ramotswe found this puzzling, and, as ever when puzzled, she decided to turn to that first line of information and consolation on all matters of doubt or dispute: the Botswana Book Centre.

She breakfasted quickly, leaving the children to be cared for by Rose. She would have liked to give them some attention, but her life now seemed unduly complicated. Dealing with Mr J.L.B. Matekoni had moved to the top of her list of tasks, followed by the garage, the investigation into the Government Man's brother's difficulties, and the move to the new office. It was a difficult list: every task on it had an element of urgency and yet there was a limited number of hours in her day.

She drove the short distance into town and found a good parking place for the tiny white van behind the Standard Bank. Then, greeting one or two known faces in the square, she made her way to the doors of the Botswana Book Centre. It was her favourite shop in town, and she usually allowed herself a good hour for the simplest purchase, which gave plenty of time for browsing the shelves; but this morning, with such a clear and worrying mission on her mind, she set her face firmly against the temptations of the magazine shelves with their pictures of improved houses and glamorous dresses.

"I would like to speak to the Manager," she said to one of the staff.

"You can speak to me," a young assistant said.

Mma Ramotswe was adamant. The assistant was polite, but very young and it would be better to speak to a man who knew a lot about books. "No," said Mma Ramotswe. "I wish to speak to the manager, Mma. This is an important matter."

The Manager was summoned, and greeted Mma Ramotswe politely.

"It is good to see you," he said. "Are you here as a detective, Mma?"

Mma Ramotswe laughed. "No, Rra. But I would like to find a book which will help me deal with a very delicate matter. May I speak to you in confidence?"

"Of course you may, Mma," he said. "You will never find a bookseller talking about the books that his customers are reading if they wish to keep it private. We are very careful."

"Good," said Mma Ramotswe. "I am looking for a book about an illness called depression. Have you heard of such a book?"

The Manager nodded. "Do not worry, Mma. I have not only heard of such a book, but I have one in the shop. I can sell that to you." He paused. "I am sorry about this, Mma. Depression is not a happy illness."

Mma Ramotswe looked over her shoulder. "It is not me," she said. "It is Mr J.L.B. Matekoni. I think that he is depressed."

The Manager's expression conveyed his sympathy as he led her to a shelf in the corner and extracted a thin red-covered book.

"This is a very good book on that illness," he said, handing her the book. "If you read what is written on the back cover, you will see that many people have said that this book has helped them greatly in dealing with this illness. I am very sorry about Mr J.L.B. Matekoni, by the way. I hope that this book makes him feel better."

"You are a very helpful man, Rra," she said. "Thank you. We are very lucky to have your good book shop in this country. Thank you."

She paid for the book and walked back to the tiny white van, leafing through the pages as she did so. One sentence in particular caught her eye and she stopped in her tracks to read it.

A characteristic feature of acute depressive illness is the feeling that one has done some terrible thing, perhaps incurred a debt one cannot honour or committed a crime. This is usually accompanied by a feeling of lack of worth. Needless to say, the imagined wrong was normally never committed, but no amount of reasoning will persuade the sufferer that this is so.

Mma Ramotswe reread the passage, her spirits rising gloriously as she did so. A book on depression might not normally be expected to have that effect on the reader, but it did now. Of course Mr J.L.B. Matekoni had done nothing terrible; he was, as she had known him to be, a man of unbesmirched honour. Now all that she had to do was to get him to see a doctor and be treated. She closed the book and glanced at the synopsis on the back cover. *This very treatable disease* . . . it said. This cheered her even further. She knew what she had to do, and her list, even if it had appeared that morning to be a long and complicated one, was now less mountainous, less daunting.

* * *

SHE WENT straight from the Botswana Book Centre to Tlokweng Road Speedy Motors. To her relief, the garage was open and Mma Makutsi was standing outside the office, drinking a cup of tea. The two apprentices were sitting on their oil drums, the one smoking a cigarette and the other drinking a soft drink from a can.

"It's rather early for a break," said Mma Ramotswe, glancing at the apprentices.

"Oh, Mma, we all deserve a break," said Mma Makutsi. "We have been here for two and half hours already. We all came in at six and we have been working very hard."

"Yes," said one of the apprentices. "Very hard. And we have done some very fine work, Mma. You tell her, Mma. You tell her what you did."

"This Acting Manager is a No. 1 mechanic," interjected the other apprentice. "Even better than the boss, I think."

Mma Makutsi laughed. "You boys are too used to saying nice things to women. That will not work with me. I am here as an acting manager, not as a woman."

"But it's true, Mma," said the elder apprentice. "If she won't tell you, then I will. We had a car here, one which had been sitting for four, five days. It belongs to a senior nurse at the Princess Marina Hospital. She is a very strong woman and I would not like to have to dance with her. Ow!"

"That woman would never dance with you," snapped Mma Makutsi. "What would she be doing dancing with a greasy boy like you, when she can dance with surgeons and people like that?"

The apprentice laughed off the insult. "Anyway, when she brought the car in she said that it stopped from time to time in the middle of the traffic and she would have to wait for a while and then start it again. Then it would start again and go for a while and then stop.

"We looked at it. I tried it and it started. I drove it over to the old airport and even out on the Lobatse Road. Nothing. No stopping. But this woman said that it was always stopping. So I replaced the spark plugs and tried it again. This time it stopped right at the circle near the Golf Club. Just stopped. Then it started again. And a very funny thing happened, which that woman had told us about. The windscreen wipers came on when the car stopped. I didn't touch them.

"So, early this morning I said to Mma Makutsi here: 'This is a very strange car, Mma. It stops and then starts.'

"Mma Makutsi came and looked at the car. She looked in the engine and saw that the plugs were new and there was a new battery too. Then she opened the door and got in, and she made a face like this, see. Just like this, with her nose all turned up. And she said: 'This car smells of mice. I can tell that it has a mouse smell.'

"She began to look about. She peered under the seats and she found nothing there. Then she looked under the dash and she started to shout out to me and my brother here. She said: 'There is a nest of mice in this car. And they have eaten the insulation off the wires right here. Look.'

"So we looked at those wires, which are very important wires for a car—the ones which are connected to the ignition, and we saw that two of them were touching, or almost touching, just where the mice had gnawed off the covering. This would mean that the engine would think that the ignition was off when the wires touched and power would go to the wipers. So that is what happened. In the meantime, the mice had run out of the car because they had been found. Mma Makutsi took out their nest and threw it away. Then she bound the wires with some tape that we gave her and now the car is fixed. It has a mouse problem no longer, all because this woman is such a good detective."

"She is a mechanic detective," said the other apprentice. "She would make a man very happy, but very tired, I think. Ow!"

"Quiet," said Mma Makutsi, playfully. "You boys must get back to work. I am the Acting Manager here. I am not one of the girls you pick up in bars. Get back to your work."

Mma Ramotswe laughed. "You obviously have a talent for finding things out, Mma. Perhaps being a detective and being a mechanic are not so different after all."

They went into the office. Mma Ramotswe immediately noticed that Mma Makutsi had made a great impression on the chaos. Although Mr J.L.B. Matekoni's desk was still covered with papers, these appeared to have been sorted into piles. Bills to be sent out had been placed in one pile, while bills to be paid had been put in another. Catalogues from suppliers had been stacked on top of a filing cabinet, and car manuals had been replaced on the shelf above his desk. And at one end of the room, leaning against the wall, was a shiny white board on which Mma Makutsi had drawn two columns headed CARS IN and CARS OUT.

"They taught us at the Botswana Secretarial College," said Mma Makutsi, "that it is very important to have a system. If you have a system which tells you where you are, then you will never be lost."

"That is true," agreed Mma Ramotswe. "They obviously knew how to run a business there."

Mma Makutsi beamed with pleasure. "And there is another

thing," she said. "I think that it would be helpful if I made you a list."

"A list?"

"Yes," said Mma Makutsi, handing her a large red file. "I have put your list in there. Each day I shall bring this list up to date. You will see that there are three columns. URGENT, NOT URGENT, and FUTURE SOMETIME."

Mma Ramotswe sighed. She did not want another list, but equally she did not want to discourage Mma Makutsi, who certainly knew how to run a garage.

"Thank you, Mma," she said, opening the file. "I see that you have already started my list."

"Yes," said Mma Makutsi. "Mma Potokwane telephoned from the orphan farm. She wanted to speak to Mr J.L.B. Matekoni, but I told her that he was not here. So she said that she was going to get in touch with you anyway and could you telephone her. You'll see that I have put it in the NOT URGENT column."

"I shall phone her," said Mma Ramotswe. "It must be something to do with the children. I had better phone her straightaway."

Mma Makutsi went back to the workshop, where Mma Ramotswe heard her calling out some instructions to the apprentices. She picked up the telephone—covered, she noticed, with greasy fingerprints, and dialled the number which Mma Makutsi had written on her list. While the telephone rang, she placed a large red tick opposite the solitary item on the list.

Mma Potokwane answered.

"Very kind of you to telephone, Mma Ramotswe. I hope that the children are well?"

"They are very settled," said Mma Ramotswe.

"Good. Now, Mma, could I ask you a favour?"

Mma Ramotswe knew that this is how the orphan farm operated. It needed help, and of course everybody was prepared to help. Nobody could refuse Mma Silvia Potokwane.

"I will help you, Mma. Just tell me what it is."

"I would like you to come and drink tea with me," said Mma Potokwane. "This afternoon, if possible. There is something you should see."

"Can you not tell me what it is?"

"No, Mma," said Mma Potokwane. "It is difficult to describe over the telephone. It would be better to see for yourself."

CHAPTER NINE

AT THE ORPHAN FARM

THE ORPHAN farm was some twenty minutes' drive out of town. Mma Ramotswe had been there on several occasions, although not as frequently as Mr J.L.B. Matekoni, who paid regular visits to deal with bits and pieces of machinery that seemed always to be going wrong. There was a borehole pump in particular that required his regular attention, and then there was their minibus, the brakes of which constantly needed attention. He never begrudged them his time, and they thought highly of him, as everybody did.

Mma Ramotswe liked Mma Potokwane, to whom she was very distantly connected through her mother's side of the family. It was not uncommon to be connected to somebody in Botswana, a lesson which foreigners were quick to learn when they realised that if they made a critical remark of somebody they were inevitably speaking to that person's distant cousin.

Mma Potokwane was standing outside the office, talking to one of the staff, when Mma Ramotswe arrived. She directed the tiny white van to a visitors' parking place under a shady syringa tree, and then invited her guest inside.

"It is so hot these days, Mma Ramotswe," she said. "But I have a very powerful fan in my office. If I turn it on to its highest setting, it can blow people out of the room. It is a very useful weapon."

"I hope that you will not do that to me," said Mma Ramotswe. For a moment she had a vision of herself being blown out of Mma Potokwane's office, her skirts all about her, up into the sky where she could look down on the trees and the paths and the cattle staring up at her in astonishment.

"Of course not," said Mma Potokwane. "You're the sort of visitor I like to receive. The sort I don't like are interfering people. People who try to tell me how to be the matron of an orphan farm. Sometimes we get these people. People who stick their noses in. They think they know about orphans, but they don't. The people who know the most about orphans are those ladies out there." She pointed out of her window, to where two of the housemothers, stout women in blue housecoats, were taking two toddlers for a walk along a path, the tiny hands firmly grasped, the hesitant, wobbly steps gently encouraged.

"Yes," went on Mma Potokwane. "Those ladies know. They can deal with any sort of child. A very sad child, who cries for its late mother all the time. A very wicked child, who has been taught to steal. A very cheeky child who has not learned to respect its elders and who uses bad words. Those ladies can deal with all those children."

"They are very good women," said Mma Ramotswe. "The

two orphans whom Mr J.L.B. Matekoni and I took say that they were very happy here. Only yesterday, Motholeli read me a story which she had written at school. The story of her life. She referred to you, Mma."

"I am glad that she was happy here," said Mma Potokwane. "She is a very brave girl, that one." She paused. "But I did not ask you out here to talk about those children, Mma. I wanted to tell you about a very strange thing that has happened here. It is so strange that even the housemothers cannot deal with it. That is why I thought that I would ask you. I was phoning Mr J.L.B. Matekoni to get your number."

She reached across her desk and poured Mma Ramotswe a cup of tea. Then she cut into a large fruitcake which was on a plate to the side of the tea tray. "This cake is made by our senior girls," she said. "We train them to cook."

Mma Ramotswe accepted her large slice of cake and looked at the rich fruit within it. There were at least seven hundred calories in that, she thought, but it did not matter; she was a traditionally built lady and she did not have to worry about such things.

"You know that we take all sorts of children," continued Mma Potokwane. "Usually they are brought to us when the mother dies and nobody knows who the father is. Often the grandmother cannot cope, because she is too ill or too poor, and then the children have nobody. We get them from the social work people or from the police sometimes. Sometimes they might just be left somewhere and a member of the public gets in touch with us."

"They are lucky to get here," said Mma Ramotswe.

"Yes. And usually, whatever has happened to them in the past, we have seen something like it before. Nothing shocks us. But every now and then a very unusual case comes in and we don't know what to do."

"And there is such a child now?"

"Yes," said Mma Potokwane. "After you have finished eating that big piece of cake I will take you and show you a boy who arrived with no name. If they have no name, we always give them one. We find a good Botswana name and they get that. But that is usually only with babies. Older children normally tell us their names. This boy didn't. In fact, he doesn't seem to have learned how to speak at all. So we decided to call him Mataila."

Mma Ramotswe finished her cake and drained the dregs of her tea. Then, together with Mma Potokwane, she walked over to one of the houses at the very edge of the circle of buildings in which the orphans lived. There were beans growing there, and the small yard in front of the door was neatly swept. This was a housemother who knew how to keep a house, thought Mma Ramotswe. And if that was the case, then how could she be defeated by a mere boy?

The housemother, Mma Kerileng, was in the kitchen. Drying her hands on her apron, she greeted Mma Ramotswe warmly and invited the two women into the living room. This was a cheerfully decorated room, with pictures drawn by the children pinned up on a large notice board. A box in one corner was filled with toys.

Mma Kerileng waited until her guests were seated before she lowered herself into one of the bulky armchairs which were arranged around a low central table.

"I have heard of you, Mma," she said to Mma Ramotswe. "I have seen your picture in the newspaper. And of course I have met Mr J.L.B. Matekoni when he has been out here fixing all the machines that are always breaking. You are a lucky lady to be marrying a man who can fix things. Most husbands just break things."

Mma Ramotswe inclined her head at the compliment. "He is a good man," she said. "He is not well at the moment, but I am hoping that he will be better very soon."

"I hope so too," said Mma Kerileng. She looked expectantly at Mma Potokwane.

"I wanted Mma Ramotswe to see Mataila," she said. "She may be able to advise us. How is he today?"

"It is the same as yesterday," said Mma Kerileng. "And the day before that. There is no change in that boy."

Mma Potokwane sighed. "It is very sad. Is he sleeping now? Can you open the door?"

"I think that he's awake," said the housemother. "Let us see anyway."

She arose from her chair and led them down a highly polished corridor. Mma Ramotswe noticed, with approval, how clean the house was. She knew how much hard work there would be in this woman; throughout the country there were women who worked and worked and who were rarely given any praise. Politicians claimed the credit for building Botswana, but how dare they? How dare they claim the credit for all the hard work of people like Mma Kerileng, and women like her.

They stopped outside a door at the end of the corridor and Mma Kerileng took a key out of her housecoat pocket.

"I cannot remember when we last locked a child in a room," she said. "In fact, I think it has never happened before. We have never had to do such a thing."

The observation seemed to make Mma Potokwane feel

uncomfortable. "There is no other way," she said. "He would run off into the bush."

"Of course," said Mma Kerileng. "It just seems very sad."

She pushed the door open, to reveal a room furnished only with a mattress. There was no glass in the window, which was covered with a large latticework wrought-iron screen of the sort used as burglar bars. Sitting on the mattress, his legs splayed out before him, was a boy of five or six, completely naked.

The boy looked at the women as they entered and for a brief moment Mma Ramotswe saw an expression of fear, of the sort one might see in the eyes of a frightened animal. But this lasted only for a short time before it was replaced by a look of vacancy, or absence.

"Mataila," said Mma Potokwane, speaking very slowly in Setswana. "Mataila, how are you today? This lady here is called Mma Ramotswe. Ramotswe. Can you see her?"

The boy looked up at Mma Potokwane as she spoke, and his gaze remained with her until she stopped speaking. Then he looked down at the floor again.

"I don't think he understands," said Mma Potokwane. "But we speak to him anyway."

"Have you tried other languages?" asked Mma Ramotswe.

Mma Potokwane nodded. "Everything we can think of. We had somebody come out from the Department of African Languages at the university. They tried some of the rarer ones, just in case he had wandered down from Zambia. We tried Herero. We tried San, although he's obviously not a Mosarwa to look at. Nothing. Absolutely nothing."

Mma Ramotswe took a step forward to get a closer look at

the boy. He raised his head slightly, but did nothing else. She stepped forward again.

"Be careful," said Mma Potokwane. "He bites. Not always, but quite often."

Mma Ramotswe stood still. Biting was a not uncommon method of fighting in Botswana, and it would not be surprising to find a child that bit. There had been a recent case reported in Mmegi of assault by biting. A waiter had bitten a customer after an argument over shortchanging, and this had led to a prosecution in the Lobatse Magistrate's Court. The waiter had been sentenced to one month's imprisonment and had immediately bitten the policeman who was leading him off to the cells; a further example, thought Mma Ramotswe, of the shortsightedness of violent people. This second bite had cost him another three months in prison.

Mma Ramotswe looked down at the child.

"Mataila?"

The boy did nothing.

"Mataila?" She stretched out towards the boy, ready to withdraw her hand sharply if necessary.

The boy growled. There was no other word for it, she thought. It was a growl, a low, guttural sound that seemed to come from his chest.

"Did you hear that?" asked Mma Potokwane. "Isn't that extraordinary? And if you're wondering why he's naked, it's because he ripped up the clothes we gave him. He ripped them with his teeth and threw them down on the ground. We gave him two pairs of shorts, and he did the same thing to both of them."

Mma Potokwane now moved forward.

"Now, Mataila," she said. "You get up and come outside. Mma Kerileng will take you out for some fresh air."

She reached down and took the boy, gingerly, by the arm. His head turned for a moment, and Mma Ramotswe thought that he was about to bite, but he did not and he meekly rose to his feet and allowed himself to be led out of the room.

Outside the house, Mma Kerileng took the boy's hand and walked with him towards a clump of trees at the edge of the compound. The boy walked with a rather unusual gait, observed Mma Ramotswe, between a run and a walk, as if he might suddenly bound off.

"So that's our Mataila," said Mma Potokwane, as they watched the housemother walk off with her charge. "What do you think of that?"

Mma Ramotswe grimaced. "It is very strange. Something terrible must have happened to that child."

"No doubt," said Mma Potokwane. "I said that to the doctor who looked at him. He said maybe yes, maybe no. He said that there are some children who are just like that. They keep to themselves and they never learn to talk."

Mma Ramotswe watched as Mma Kerileng briefly let go of the child's hand.

"We have to watch him all the time," said Mma Potokwane. "If we leave him, he runs off into the bush and hides. He went missing for four hours last week. They eventually found him over by the sewerage ponds. He does not seem to know that a naked child running as fast as he can is likely to attract attention."

Mma Potokwane and Mma Ramotswe began to walk back together towards the office. Mma Ramotswe felt depressed. She wondered how one would make a start with a child like that. It was easy to respond to the needs of appealing orphans—of children such as the two who had come to live in Zebra Drive—but there were so many other children, children who had been damaged in some way or other, and who would need patience and understanding. She contemplated her life, with its lists and its demands, and she wondered how she would ever find the time to be the mother of a child like that. Surely Mma Potokwane could not be planning that she and Mr J.L.B. Matekoni should take this child too? She knew that the matron had a reputation for determination and for not taking no for an answer—which of course made her a powerful advocate for her orphans—but she could not imagine that she would try to impose in this way, for in any view it would be a great imposition to foist this child off on her.

"I am a busy woman," she started to say, as they neared the office. "I'm sorry, but I cannot take . . ."

A group of orphans walked past them and greeted the matron politely. They had with them a small, undernourished puppy, which one of them was cradling in her arms; one orphan helps another, thought Mma Ramotswe.

"Be careful with that dog," warned Mma Potokwane. "I am always telling you that you should not pick up these strays. Will you not listen . . ."

She turned to Mma Ramotswe. "But Mma Ramotswe! I hope that you did not think . . . Of course I did not expect you to take that boy! We can barely manage him here, with all our resources."

"I was worried," said Mma Ramotswe. "I am always prepared to help, but there is a limit to what I can do."

Mma Potokwane laughed, and touched her guest reassuringly on the forearm. "Of course you are. You are already helping us by taking those two orphans. No, I wanted only to ask your advice. I know that you have a very good reputation for finding missing people. Could you tell us—just tell us—how we might find out about this boy? If we could somehow discover something about his past, about where he came from, we might be able to get through to him."

Mma Ramotswe shook her head. "It will be too difficult. You would have to talk to people near where he was found. You would have to ask a lot of questions, and I think that people will not want to talk. If they did, they would have said something."

"You are right about that," said Mma Potokwane sadly. "The police asked a lot of questions up there, outside Maun. They asked in all the local villages, and nobody knew of a child like that. They showed his photograph and people just said no. They knew nothing of him."

Mma Ramotswe was not surprised. If anybody wanted the child, then somebody would have said something. The fact that there was a silence probably meant that the child had been deliberately abandoned. And there was always the possibility of some sort of witchcraft with a child like that. If a local spirit doctor had said that the child was possessed, or was a tokolosi, then nothing could be done for him: he was probably fortunate to be alive. Such children often met a quite different fate.

They were now standing beside the tiny white van. The tree had shed a frond on the vehicle's top, and Mma Ramotswe picked it up. They were so delicate, the leaves of this tree; with their hundreds of tiny leaves attached to the central stem, like the intricate tracing of a spider's web. Behind them was the sound of children's voices; a song which Mma Ramotswe remembered from her own childhood, and which made her smile.

The cattle come home, one, two, three,
The cattle come home, the big one, the small one, the one with one horn,
I live with the cattle, one, two, three,
Oh mother, look out for me.

She looked into Mma Potokwane's face; a face which said, in every line and in every expression: I am the matron of an orphan farm.

"They are still singing that song," said Mma Ramotswe.

Mma Potokwane smiled. "I sing it too. We never forget the songs of our childhood, do we?"

"Tell me," said Mma Ramotswe. "What did they say about that boy? Did the people who found him say anything?"

Mma Potokwane thought for a moment. "They told the police that they found him in the dark. They said that he was very difficult to control. And they said that he had a strange smell about him."

"What strange smell?"

Mma Potokwane made a dismissive gesture with a hand. "One of the men said that he smelled of lion. The policeman remembered it because it was such a strange thing to say. He wrote it down in his report, which came to us eventually when the tribal administration people up there sent the boy down to us."

"Like lion?" asked Mma Ramotswe.

"Yes," said Mma Potokwane. "Ridiculous."

Mma Ramotswe said nothing for a moment. She climbed

into the tiny white van and thanked Mma Potokwane for her hospitality.

"I shall think about this boy," she said. "Maybe I shall be able to come up with an idea."

They waved to one another as Mma Ramotswe drove down the dusty road, through the orphanage gates, with their large ironwork sign proclaiming: Children live here.

She drove slowly, as there were donkeys and cattle on the road, and the herd boys who looked after them. Some of the herd boys were very young, no more than six or seven, like that poor, silent boy in his little room.

What if a young herd boy got lost, thought Mma Ramotswe. What if he got lost in the bush, far from the cattle post? Would he die? Or might something else happen to him?

CHAPTER TEN

THE CLERK'S TALE

MMA RAMOTSWE realised that something would have to be done about the No. 1 Ladies' Detective Agency. It did not take long to move the contents of the old office to the new quarters at the back of Tlokweng Road Speedy Motors; there was not much more than one filing cabinet and its contents, a few metal trays in which papers awaiting filing could be placed, the old teapot and its two chipped mugs, and of course the old typewriter—which had been given to her by Mr J.L.B. Matekoni and was now going home. These were manhandled into the back of the tiny white van by the two apprentices, after only the most token complaint that this was not part of their job. It would appear that they would do anything requested of them by Mma Makutsi, who had only to whistle from the office to find one of them running in to find out what she needed.

This compliance was a surprise to Mma Ramotswe, and she wondered what it was that Mma Makutsi had over these two young men. Mma Makutsi was not beautiful in a conventional sense. Her skin was too dark for modern tastes, thought Mma Ramotswe, and the lightening cream that she used had left patches. Then there was her hair, which was often braided, but braided in a very strange way. And then there were her glasses, of course, with their large lenses that would have served the needs of at least two people, in Mma Ramotswe's view. Yet here was this person who would never have got into round one of a beauty competition, commanding the slavish attentions of these two notoriously difficult young men. It was very puzzling.

It could be, of course, that there was something more than mere physical appearance behind this. Mma Makutsi may not have been a great beauty, but she certainly had a powerful personality, and perhaps these boys recognised that. Beauty queens were often devoid of character, and men must surely tire of that after a while. Those dreadful competitions which they held—the *Miss Lovers Special Time Competition* or the *Miss Cattle Industry Competition*—brought to the fore the most vacuous of girls. These vacuous girls then attempted to pronounce on all sorts of issues, and to Mma Ramotswe's utter incomprehension, they were often listened to.

She knew that these young men followed the beauty competitions, for she had heard them talking about them. But now their main concern seemed to be to impress Mma Makutsi, and to flatter her. One had even attempted to kiss her, and had been pushed away with amused indignation.

"Since when does a mechanic kiss the manager?" asked

Mma Makutsi. "Get back to work before I beat your useless bottom with a big stick."

The apprentices had made short work of the move, loading the entire contents within half an hour. Then, with the two young men travelling in the back to hold the filing cabinet in place, the No. 1 Ladies' Detective Agency, complete with painted sign, made its way to its new premises. It was a sad moment, and both Mma Ramotswe and Mma Makutsi were close to tears as they locked the front door for the last time.

"It is just a move, Mma," said Mma Makutsi, in an attempt to comfort her employer. "It is not as if we are going out of business."

"I know," said Mma Ramotswe, looking, for the last time perhaps, at the view from the front of the building, over the rooftops of the town and the tops of the thorn trees. "I have been very happy here."

We are still in business. Yes, but only just. Over the last few days, with all the turmoil and the lists, Mma Ramotswe had devoted very little time to the affairs of the agency. In fact, she had devoted no time at all, when she came to think about it. There was only one outstanding case, and nothing else had come in, although it undoubtedly would. She would be able to charge the Government Man a proper fee for her time, but that would depend on a successful outcome. She could send him an account even if she found nothing, but she always felt embarrassed asking for payment when she was unable to help the client. Perhaps she would just have to steel herself to do this in the Government Man's case, as he was a wealthy man and could well afford to pay. It must be very easy, she thought, to have a detective agency that catered only to the needs of rich people, the No. 1 Rich Person's Detective Agency, as the charging of fees would always be painless. But that was not what her business was, and she was not sure that she would be happy with that. Mma Ramotswe liked to help everybody, no matter what their station was in life. She had often been out of pocket on a case, simply because she could not refuse to help a person in need. This is what I am called to do, she said to herself. I must help whomsoever asks for my help. That is my duty: to help other people with the problems in their lives. Not that you could do everything. Africa was full of people in need of help and there had to be a limit. You simply could not help everybody; but you could at least help those who came into your life. That principle allowed you to deal with the suffering you saw. That was your suffering. Other people would have to deal with the suffering that they, in their turn, came across.

BUT WHAT to do, here and now, with the problems of the business? Mma Ramotswe decided that she would have to revise her list and put the Government Man's case at the top. This meant that she should start making enquiries immediately, and where better to start than with the suspect wife's father? There were several reasons for this, the most important being that if there really were a plot to dispose of the Government Man's brother, then this would probably not be the wife's idea, but would have been dreamed up by the father. Mma Ramotswe was convinced that people who got up to really serious mischief very rarely acted entirely on their own initiative. There was usually somebody else involved, somebody who would stand to benefit in some way, or somebody close to the perpetrator of the deed who was brought in for moral support. In this case, the most likely person would be the wife's father. If, as the Government Man had implied, this man was aware of the social betterment which the marriage entailed, and made much of it, then he was likely to be socially ambitious himself. And in that case, it would be highly convenient for him to have the son-in-law out of the way, so that he could, through his daughter, lay hands on a substantial part of the family assets. Indeed, the more Mma Ramotswe thought about it, the more likely it seemed that the poisoning attempt was the clerk's idea.

She could imagine his thoughts, as he sat at his small government desk and reflected on the power and authority which he saw all about him and of which he had only such a small part. How galling it must be for a man of this stripe to see the Government Man drive past him in his official car; the Government Man who was, in fact, the brother-in-law of his own daughter. How difficult it must be for him not to have the recognition that he undoubtedly felt that he would get if only more people knew that he was connected in such a way with such a family. If the money and the cattle came to him—or to his daughter, which amounted to the same thing—then he would be able to give up his demeaning post in the civil service and pursue the life of a rich farmer; he, who now had no cattle, would have cattle aplenty. He, who now had to scrimp and save in order to afford a trip up to Francistown each year, would be able to eat meat every day and drink Lion Lager with his friends on Friday evenings, generously buying rounds for all. And all that stood between him and all this was one small, beating heart. If that heart could be silenced, then his entire life would be transformed.

The Government Man had given Mma Ramotswe the wife's

family name and had told her that the father liked to spend his lunch hour sitting under a tree outside the Ministry. This gave her all the information she needed to find him: his name and his tree.

"I am going to begin this new case," she said to Mma Makutsi, as the two of them sat in their new office. "You are busy with the garage. I shall get back to being a detective."

"Good," said Mma Makutsi. "It is a demanding business running a garage. I shall continue to be very busy."

"I am glad to see that the apprentices are working so hard," said Mma Ramotswe. "You have them eating out of your hand."

Mma Makutsi smiled conspiratorially. "They are very silly young men," she said. "But we ladies are used to dealing with silly young men."

"So I see," said Mma Ramotswe. "You must have had many boyfriends, Mma. These boys seem to like you."

Mma Makutsi shook her head. "I have had almost no boyfriends. I cannot understand why these boys are like this to me when there are all these pretty girls in Gaborone."

"You underestimate yourself, Mma," said Mma Ramotswe. "You are obviously an attractive lady to men."

"Do you think so?" asked Mma Makutsi, beaming with pleasure.

"Yes," said Mma Ramotswe. "Some ladies become more attractive to men the older they get. I have seen this happen. Then, while all the young girls, the beauty queens, get less and less attractive as they get older, these other ladies become more and more so. It is a very interesting thing."

Mma Makutsi looked thoughtful. She adjusted her glasses, and Mma Ramotswe noticed her glancing surreptitiously at her reflection in the window pane. She was not sure if what she had said was true, but even if it were not, she would be glad that she had said it if it had the effect of boosting Mma Makutsi's confidence. It would do her no harm at all to be admired by these two feckless boys, as long as she did not get involved with them, and it was clear to Mma Ramotswe that there was little chance of that—at least for the time being.

She left Mma Makutsi in the office and drove off in the tiny white van. It was now half past twelve; the drive would take ten minutes, which would give her time to find a parking place and to make her way to the Ministry and to start looking for the wife's father, Mr Kgosi Sipoleli, ministry clerk and, if her intuitions were correct, would-be murderer.

She parked the tiny white van near the Catholic church, as the town was busy and there were no places to be had any closer. She would have a walk—a brief one—and she did not mind this, as she was bound to see people whom she knew and she had a few minutes in hand for a chat on her way.

She was not disappointed. Barely had she turned the corner from her parking place than she ran into Mma Gloria Bopedi, mother of Chemba Bopedi, who had been at school with Mma Ramotswe in Mochudi. Chemba had married Pilot Matanyani, who had recently become headmaster of a school at Selibi-Pikwe. She had seven children, the oldest of whom had recently become champion under-fifteen sprinter of Botswana.

"How is your very fast grandson, Mma?" asked Mma Ramotswe.

The elderly woman beamed. She had few teeth left, noticed Mma Ramotswe, who thought that it would be better for her to have the remaining ones out and be fitted with false teeth.

"Oh! He is fast, that one," said Mma Bopedi. "But he is a naughty boy too. He learned to run fast so that he could get out of trouble. That is how he came to be so fast."

"Well," said Mma Ramotswe, "something good has come out of it. Maybe he will be in the Olympics one day, running for Botswana. That will show the world that the fast runners are not all in Kenya."

Again she found herself reflecting on the fact that what she said was not true. The truth of the matter was that the best runners did all come from Kenya, where the people were very tall and had long legs, very suitably designed for running. The problem with the Batswana was that they were not very tall. Their men tended to be stocky, which was fine for looking after cattle, but which did not lend itself to athleticism. Indeed, most Southern Africans were not very good runners, although the Zulus and the Swazis sometimes produced somebody who made a mark on the track, such as that great Swazi runner, Richard "Concorde" Mavuso.

Of course, the Boers were quite good at sports. They produced these very large men with great thighs and thick necks, like Brahman cattle. They played rugby and seemed to do very well at it, although they were not very bright. She preferred a Motswana man, who may not be as big as one of those rugby players, nor as swift as one of those Kenyan runners, but at least he would be reliable and astute.

"Don't you think so, Mma?" she said to Mma Bopedi.

"Don't I think what, Mma?" asked Mma Bopedi.

Mma Ramotswe realised that she had included the other woman in her reverie, and apologised.

"I was just thinking about our men," she said.

Mma Bopedi raised an eyebrow. "Oh, really, Mma? Well, to tell you the truth, I also think about our men from time to time. Not very often, but sometimes. You know how it is."

Mma Ramotswe bade Mma Bopedi farewell and continued with her journey. Now, outside the optician's shop, she came across Mr Motheti Pilai, standing quite still, looking up at the sky.

"Dumela, Rra," she said politely. "Are you well?"

Mr Pilai looked down. "Mma Ramotswe," he said. "Please let me look at you. I have just been given these new spectacles, and I can see the world clearly for the first time in years. Ow! It is a wonderful thing. I had forgotten what it was like to see clearly. And there you are, Mma. You are looking very beautiful, very fat."

"Thank you, Rra."

He moved the spectacles to the end of his nose. "My wife was always telling me that I needed new glasses, but I was always afraid to come here. I do not like that machine that he has which shines light into your eyes. And I do not like that machine which puffs air into your eyeball. So I put it off and put it off. I was very foolish."

"It is never a good thing to put something off," said Mma Ramotswe, thinking of how she had put off the Government Man's case.

"Oh, I know that," said Mr Pilai. "But the problem is that even if you know that is the best thing to do, you often don't do it."

"That is very puzzling," said Mma Ramotswe. "But it is true. It's as if there were two people inside you. One says: do this. Another says: do that. But both these voices are inside the same person."

Mr Pilai stared at Mma Ramotswe. "It is very hot today," he said.

She agreed with him, and they both went about their business. She would stop no more, she resolved; it was now almost one o'clock and she wanted to have enough time to locate Mr Sipoleli and to have the conversation with him that would start her enquiry.

THE TREE was easily identified. It stood a short distance from the main entrance to the Ministry, a large acacia tree with a wide canopy that provided a wide circle of shade on the dusty ground below. Immediately beside the trunk were several strategically placed stones—comfortable seats for anyone who might wish to sit under the tree and watch the daily business of Gaborone unfold before him. Now, at five minutes to one, the stones were unoccupied.

Mma Ramotswe chose the largest of the stones and settled herself upon it. She had brought with her a large flask of tea, two aluminum mugs, and four corned beef sandwiches made with thickly cut slices of bread. She took out one of the mugs and filled it with bush tea. Then she leaned back against the trunk of the tree and waited. It was pleasant to be seated there in the shade, with a mug of tea, watching the passing traffic. Nobody paid the slightest attention to her, as it was an entirely normal thing to see: a well-built woman under a tree.

Shortly after ten past one, when Mma Ramotswe had finished her tea and was on the point of dozing off in her comfortable place, a figure emerged from the front of the Ministry and walked over towards the tree. As he drew near, Mma

Ramotswe jolted herself to full wakefulness. She was on duty now, and she must make the most of the opportunity to talk to Mr Sipoleli, if that, as she expected, was the person now approaching her.

The man was wearing a pair of neatly pressed blue trousers, a short-sleeved white shirt, and a dark brown tie. It was exactly what one would expect a junior civil servant, in the clerical grade, to wear. And as if to confirm the diagnosis, there was a row of pens tucked neatly into his shirt pocket. This was clearly the uniform of the junior clerk, even if it was being worn by a man in his late forties. This, then, was a clerk who was stuck where he was and was not going any further.

The man approached the tree cautiously. Staring at Mma Ramotswe, it seemed as if he wanted to say something but could not quite bring himself to speak.

Mma Ramotswe smiled at him. "Good afternoon, Rra," she said. "It is hot today, is it not? That is why I am under this tree. It is clearly a good place to sit in the heat."

The man nodded. "Yes," he said. "I normally sit here."

Mma Ramotswe affected surprise. "Oh? I hope that I am not sitting on your rock, Rra. I found it here and there was nobody sitting on it."

He made an impatient gesture with his hands. "My rock? Yes it is, as a matter of fact. That is my rock. But this is a public place and anybody can sit on it, I suppose."

Mma Ramotswe rose to her feet. "But Rra, you must have this rock. I shall sit on that one over on that side."

"No, Mma," he said hurriedly, his tone changing. "I do not want to inconvenience you. I can sit on that rock."

"No. You sit on this rock here. It is your rock. I would not have sat on it if I had thought that it was another person's rock. I can sit on this rock, which is a good rock too. You sit on that rock."

"No," he said firmly. "You go back where you were, Mma. I can sit on that rock any day. You can't. I shall sit on this rock."

Mma Ramotswe, with a show of reluctance, returned to her original rock, while Mr Sipoleli settled himself down.

"I am drinking tea, Rra," she said. "But I have enough for you. I would like you to have some, since I am sitting on your rock."

Mr Sipoleli smiled. "You are very kind, Mma. I love to drink tea. I drink a lot of tea in my office. I am a civil servant, you see."

"Oh?" said Mma Ramotswe. "That is a good job. You must be important."

Mr Sipoleli laughed. "No," he said. "I am not at all important. I am a junior clerk. But I am lucky to be that. There are people with degrees being recruited into my level of job. I have my Cambridge Certificate, that is all. I feel that I have done well enough."

Mma Ramotswe listened to this as she poured his tea. She was surprised by what she had heard; she had expected a rather different sort of person, a minor official puffed up with his importance and eager for greater status. Here, by contrast, was a man who seemed to be quite content with what he was and where he had got himself.

"Could you not be promoted, Rra? Would it not be possible to go further up?"

Mr Sipoleli considered her question carefully. "I suppose it would," he said after a few moments' thought. "The problem is that I would have to spend a lot of time getting on the right side of more senior people. Then I would have to say the right things and write bad reports on my juniors. That is not what I would like to do. I am not an ambitious man. I am happy where I am, really I am."

Mma Ramotswe's hand faltered in the act of passing him his tea. This was not at all what she had expected, and suddenly she remembered Clovis Andersen's words of advice. Never make any prior assumptions, he had written. Never decide in advance what's what or who's who. This may set you off on the wrong track altogether.

She decided to offer him a sandwich, which she pulled out of her plastic bag. He was pleased, but chose the smallest of the sandwiches; another indication, she thought, of a modest personality. The Mr Sipoleli of her imagining would have taken the largest sandwich without hesitation.

"Do you have family in Gaborone, Rra?" she asked innocently.

Mr Sipoleli finished his mouthful of corned beef before answering. "I have three daughters," he said. "Two are nurses, one at the Princess Marina and the other out at Molepolole. Then there is my firstborn, who did very well at school and went to the university. We are very proud of her."

"She lives in Gaborone?" asked Mma Ramotswe, passing him another sandwich.

"No," he replied. "She is living somewhere else. She married a young man she met while she was studying. They live out that way. Over there."

"And this son-in-law of yours," said Mma Ramotswe. "What about him? Is he good to her?"

"Yes," said Mr Sipoleli. "He is a very good man. They are very happy, and I hope that they have many children. I am looking forward to being a grandfather."

Mma Ramotswe thought for a moment. Then she said: "The best thing about seeing one's children married must be the thought that they will be able to look after you when you are old."

Mr Sipoleli smiled. "Well, that is probably true. But in my case, my wife and I have different plans. We intend to go back to Mahalapye. I have some cattle there—just a few—and some lands. We will be happy up there. That is all we want."

Mma Ramotswe was silent. This patently good man was obviously telling the truth. Her suspicion that he could be behind a plot to kill his son-in-law was an absurd conclusion to have reached, and she felt thoroughly ashamed of herself. To hide her confusion, she offered him another cup of tea, which he accepted gratefully. Then, after fifteen minutes of further conversation about matters of the day, she stood up, dusted down her skirt, and thanked him for sharing his lunch hour with her. She had found out what she wanted to know, at least about him. But the meeting with the father also threw some doubt on her surmises as to the daughter. If the daughter was at all like the father, then she could not possibly be a poisoner. This good unassuming man was unlikely to have raised a daughter who would do a thing like that. Or was he? It was always possible for bad children to spring from the loins of good parents; it did not require much experience of life to realise that. Yet, at the same time, it tended to be unlikely, and this meant that the next stage of the investigation would require a considerably more open mind than had characterised the initial stage.

I have learned a lesson, Mma Ramotswe told herself as she walked back to the tiny white van. She was deep in thought, and she barely noticed Mr Pilai, still standing outside the optician's shop, gazing at the branches of the tree above his head.

"I have been thinking about what you said to me, Mma," he remarked, as she walked past. "It was a very thought-provoking remark."

"Yes," said Mma Ramotswe, slightly taken aback. "And I am afraid I do not know what the answer is. I simply do not."

Mr Pilai shook his head. "Then we shall have to think about it some more," he said.

"Yes," said Mma Ramotswe. "We shall."

CHAPTER ELEVEN

MMA POTOKWANE OBLIGES

THE GOVERNMENT Man had given Mma Ramotswe a telephone number which she could use at any time and which would circumvent his secretaries and assistants. That afternoon she tried the number for the first time, and got straight through to her client. He sounded pleased to hear from her, and expressed his pleasure that the investigation had begun.

"I would like to go down to the house next week," said Mma Ramotswe. "Have you contacted your father?"

"I have done that," said the Government Man. "I have told him that you will be coming to stay for a rest. I told him that you have found many votes for me amongst the women and that I must repay you. You will be well looked after."

Details were agreed, and Mma Ramotswe was given directions to the farm, which lay off the Francistown Road, to the north of Pilane.

"I am sure that you will find evidence of wickedness," said the Government Man. "Then we can save my poor brother."

Mma Ramotswe was noncommittal. "We shall see. I can't guarantee anything. I shall have to see."

"Of course, Mma," the Government Man said hurriedly. "But I have complete confidence in your ability to find out what is happening. I know that you will be able to find evidence against that wicked woman. Let's just hope that you are in time."

After the telephone call, Mma Ramotswe sat at her desk and stared at the wall. She had just taken a whole week out of her diary, and that meant that all the other tasks on her list were consigned to an uncertain future. At least she need not worry about the garage for the time being, nor indeed need she worry about dealing with enquiries at the agency. Mma Makutsi could do all that and if, as was increasingly often the case these days, she was under a car at the time, then the apprentices had been trained to answer the telephone on her behalf.

But what about Mr J.L.B. Matekoni? That was the one really difficult issue which remained untouched, and she realised that she would have to do something quickly. She had finished reading the book on depression and she now felt more confident in dealing with its puzzling symptoms. But there was always a danger with that illness that the sufferer might do something rash—the book had been quite explicit about that—and she dreaded the thought of Mr J.L.B. Matekoni being driven to such extremes by his feelings of lowness and self-disesteem. She would have to get him to Dr Moffat somehow, so that treatment could begin. But when she had told him that he was to see a doctor, he had flatly refused. If she tried again, she would probably get the same response.

She wondered whether there was any way of getting him to take the pills by trickery. She did not like the idea of using underhand methods with Mr J.L.B. Matekoni, but when a person's reason was disturbed, then she thought that any means were justified in getting them better. It was as if a person had been kidnapped by some evil being and held ransom. You would not hesitate, she felt, to resort to trickery to defeat the evil being. In her view, that was perfectly in line with the old Botswana morality, or indeed with any other sort of morality.

She had wondered whether she could conceal the tablets in his food. This might have been possible if she had been attending to his every meal, but she was not. He had stopped coming round to her house for his evening meal, and it would look very strange if she suddenly arrived at his house to cater for him. Anyway, she suspected that he was not eating very much in his state of depression—the book had warned about this—as he appeared to be losing weight quite markedly. It would be impossible, then, to administer the drugs to him in this way, even if she decided that this was the proper thing to do.

She sighed. It was unlike her to sit and stare at a wall, and for a moment the thought crossed her mind that she, too, might be becoming depressed. But the thought passed quickly; it would be out of the question for Mma Ramotswe to become ill. Everything depended on her: the garage, the agency, the children, Mr J.L.B Matekoni, Mma Makutsi—not to mention Mma Makutsi's people up in Bobonong. She simply could not afford the time to be ill. So she rose to her feet, straightened her dress, and made her way to the telephone on the other side of the room. She took out the small book in which she noted down telephone numbers. Potokwane, Silvia. Matron. Orphan Farm.

MMA POTOKWANE was interviewing a prospective foster parent when Mma Ramotswe arrived. Sitting in the waiting room, Mma Ramotswe watched a small, pale gecko stalk a fly on the ceiling above her head. Both the gecko and the fly were upside down; the gecko relying on minute suction pads on each of its toes, the fly on its spurs. The gecko suddenly darted forward, but was too slow for the fly, which launched itself into a victory roll before settling on the windowsill.

Mma Ramotswe turned to the magazines that littered the table. There was a Government brochure with a picture of senior officials. She looked at the faces—she knew many of these people, and in one or two cases knew rather more about them than would be published in Government brochures. And there was the face of her Government Man, smiling confidently into the camera, while all the time, as she knew, he was eaten up by anxiety for his younger brother and imagining plots against his life. "Mma Ramotswe?"

Mma Potokwane had ushered the foster parent out and now stood looking down on Mma Ramotswe. "I'm sorry to have kept you waiting, Mma, but I think I have found a home for a very difficult child. I had to make sure that the woman was the right sort of person."

They went into the matron's room, where a crumb-littered plate bore witness to the last serving of fruitcake.

"You have come about the boy?" asked Mma Potokwane. "You must have had an idea."

Mma Ramotswe shook her head. "Sorry, Mma. I have not had time to think about that boy. I have been very busy with other things."

Mma Potokwane smiled. "You are always a busy person."

"I've come to ask you a favour," said Mma Ramotswe.

"Ah!" Mma Potokwane was beaming with pleasure. "Usually it is I who do that. Now it is different, and I am pleased."

"Mr J.L.B. Matekoni is ill," explained Mma Ramotswe. "I think that he has an illness called depression."

"Ow!" interrupted Mma Potokwane. "I know all about that. Remember that I used to be a nurse. I spent a year working at the mental hospital at Lobatse. I have seen what that illness can do. But at least it can be treated these days. You can get better from depression."

"I have read that," said Mma Ramotswe. "But you have to take the drugs. Mr J.L.B. Matekoni won't even see a doctor. He says he's not ill."

"That's nonsense," said Mma Potokwane. "He should go to the doctor immediately. You should tell him."

"I tried," said Mma Ramotswe. "He said there was nothing wrong with him. I need to get somebody to take him to the doctor. Somebody . . ."

"Somebody like me?" cut in Mma Potokwane.

"Yes," said Mma Ramotswe. "He has always done what you have asked him to do. He wouldn't dare refuse you."

"But he'll need to take the drugs," said Mma Potokwane. "I wouldn't be there to stand over him."

"Well," mused Mma Ramotswe, "if you brought him here, you could nurse him. You could make sure that he took the drugs and became better."

"You mean that I should bring him to the orphan farm?"

"Yes," said Mma Ramotswe. "Bring him here until he's better."

Mma Potokwane tapped her desk. "And if he says that he does not want to come?"

"He would not dare to contradict you, Mma," said Mma Ramotswe. "He would be too scared."

"Oh," said Mma Potokwane. "Am I like that, then?"

"A little bit," said Mma Ramotswe, gently. "But only to men. Men respect a matron."

Mma Potokwane thought for a moment. Then she spoke. "Mr J.L.B. Matekoni has been a good friend to the orphan farm. He has done a great deal for us. I will do this thing for you, Mma. When shall I go to see him?"

"Today," said Mma Ramotswe. "Take him to Dr Moffat. Then bring him right back here."

"Very well," said Mma Potokwane, warming to her task. "I shall go and find out what all this nonsense is about. Not wanting to go to the doctor? What nonsense! I shall sort all this out for you, Mma. You just trust me."

Mma Potokwane showed Mma Ramotswe to her car.

"You won't forget the boy, will you, Mma?" she asked. "You will remember to think about him?"

"Don't worry, Mma," she replied. "You have taken a big weight off my mind. Now I shall try to take one off yours."

DR MOFFAT saw Mr J.L.B. Matekoni in the study at the end of his verandah, while Mma Potokwane drank a cup of tea with Mrs Moffat in the kitchen. The doctor's wife, who was a librarian, knew a great deal, and Mma Potokwane had occasionally consulted her for pieces of information. It was evening, and in the doctor's study insects which had penetrated the fly screens were drunkenly circling the bulb of the desk lamp, throwing themselves against the shade and then, singed by the heat, fluttering wing-injured away. On the desk were a stethoscope and a sphygmomanometer, with its rubber bulb hanging over the edge; on the wall, an old engraving of Kuruman Mission in the mid-nineteenth century.

"I have not seen you for some time, Rra," Dr Moffat said. "My car has been behaving itself well."

Mr J.L.B. Matekoni started to smile, but the effort seemed to defeat him. "I have not . . ." He tailed off. Dr Moffat waited, but nothing more came.

"You have not been feeling very well?"

Mr J.L.B. Matekoni nodded. "I am very tired. I cannot sleep."

"That is very hard. If we do not sleep, then we feel bad." He paused. "Are you troubled by anything in particular? Are there things that worry you?"

Mr J.L.B. Matekoni thought. His jaws worked, as if he was trying to articulate impossible words, and then he replied. "I am worried that bad things I did a long time ago will come back. Then I shall be in disgrace. They will all throw stones at me. It will be the end."

"And these bad things? What are they? You know that you can speak to me about them and I shall not tell anybody."

"They are bad things I did a long time ago. They are very bad things. I cannot speak to anybody about them, not even you."

"And is that all you want to tell me about them?"

"Yes."

Dr Moffat watched Mr J.L.B. Matekoni. He noticed the collar, fastened at the wrong button; he saw the shoes, with their broken laces; he saw the eyes, almost lachrymose in their anguish, and he knew.

"I am going to give you some medicine that will help you to get well," he said. "Mma Potokwane out there says that she will look after you while you are getting better."

Mr J.L.B. Matekoni nodded dumbly.

"And you will promise me that you will take this medicine," Dr Moffat went on. "Will you give me your word that you will do that?"

Mr J.L.B. Matekoni's gaze, firmly fixed on the floor, did not move up. "My word is worth nothing," he said quietly.

"That is the illness speaking," Dr Moffat said gently. "Your word is worth a great deal."

MMA POTOKWANE led him to her car and opened the passenger door for him. She looked at Dr Moffat and his wife, who were standing at the gate, and she waved to them. They waved back before returning to the house. Then she drove off, back to the orphan farm, passing Tlokweng Road Speedy Motors as she did so. The garage, deserted and forlorn in the darkness, got no glance from its proprietor, its begetter, as he rode past.

CHAPTER TWELVE

FAMILY BUSINESS

SHE LEFT in the cool of the morning, although the journey would take little more than an hour. Rose had prepared breakfast, and she ate it with the children, sitting on the verandah of her house on Zebra Drive. It was a quiet time, as little traffic passed along their road before seven, when people would start to go to work. There were a few people walking by—a tall man, with shabby trousers, eating a fire-charred corn cob, a woman carrying a baby, strapped to her back with its shawl, the baby's head nodding in sleep. One of her neighbour's yellow dogs, lean and undernourished, slunk by, occupied in some mysterious, but quite purposeful canine business. Mma Ramotswe tolerated dogs, but she had a strong distaste for the foul-smelling yellow creatures that lived next door. Their howling at night disturbed her—they would bark at shadows, at the moon, at gusts of wind—and she was sure that they deterred birds, which she did like, from coming to her garden. Every house, except hers, seemed to have its quota of dogs, and occasionally these dogs, overcoming the restrictions of imposed loyalties, would rise above their mutual animosity and walk down the street in a pack, chasing cars and frightening cyclists.

Mma Ramotswe poured bush tea for herself and Motholeli; Puso refused to get used to tea and had a glass of warm milk, into which Mma Ramotswe had stirred two generous spoons of sugar. He had a sweet tooth, possibly as a result of sweet foods which his sister had given him when she was caring for him in that yard up in Francistown. She would try to wean him onto healthier things, but that change would require patience. Rose had made them porridge, which stood in bowls, dark molasses trailed across its surface, and there were sections of paw-paw on a plate. It was a healthy breakfast for a child, thought Mma Ramotswe. What would these children have eaten had they stayed with their people, she wondered? Those people survived on next to nothing; roots dug up from the ground, grubs, the eggs of birds; yet they could hunt as nobody else could, and there would have been ostrich meat and duiker, which people in towns could rarely afford.

She remembered how, when travelling north, she had stopped beside the road to enjoy a flask of tea. The stopping place was a clearing at the side of the road, where a battered sign indicated that one was at that point crossing the Tropic of Capricorn. She had thought herself alone, and had been surprised when there emerged from behind a tree a Mosarwa, or Bushman, as they used to be called. He was wearing a small leather apron and carrying a skin bag of some sort; and had approached her, whistling away in that curious language they use. For a moment she had been frightened; although she was twice his size, these people carried arrows, and poisons, and were naturally very quick.

She had risen uncertainly to her feet, ready to abandon her flask and seek the safety of the tiny white van, but he had simply pointed to his mouth in supplication. Understanding, Mma Ramotswe had passed her cup to him, but he had indicated that it was food, not drink, that he wanted. All that Mma Ramotswe had with her was a couple of egg sandwiches, which he took greedily when offered and bit into hungrily. When he had finished, he licked his fingers and turned away. She watched him as he disappeared into the bush, merging with it as naturally as would a wild creature. She wondered what he had made of the egg sandwich and whether it tasted better to him, or worse, than the offerings of the Kalahari; the rodents and tubers.

The children had belonged to that world, but there could be no going back. That was a life to which one simply could not return, because what had been taken for granted then would seem impossibly hard, and the skills would have gone. Their place now was with Rose, and Mma Ramotswe, in the house on Zebra Drive.

"I am going to have to be away for four or five days," she explained to them over breakfast. "Rose will be looking after you. You will be all right."

"That is fine, Mma," said Motholeli. "I will help her."

Mma Ramotswe smiled at her encouragingly. She had brought up her little brother, and it was in her nature to help those who were younger than she was. She would be a fine mother eventually, she thought, but then she remembered. Could she be a mother in a wheelchair? It would probably be impossible to bear a child if one could not walk, Mma Ramotswe thought, and even if it were possible, she was not sure that any man would want to marry a woman in a wheelchair. It was very unfair, but you could not hide your face from the truth. It would always be more difficult for that girl, always. Of course there were some good men around who would not think that such a thing mattered, and who would want to marry the girl for the fine, plucky person that she was, but such men were very rare, and Mma Ramotswe had trouble in thinking of many. Or did she? There was Mr J.L.B. Matekoni, of course, who was a very good man—even if temporarily a little bit odd—and there was the Bishop, and there had been Sir Seretse Khama, statesman and Paramount Chief. Dr Merriweather, who ran the Scottish Hospital at Molepolole; he was a good man. And there were others, who were less well-known, now that she came to think of it. Mr Potolani, who helped very poor people and gave away most of the money he had made from his stores; and the man who fixed her roof and who repaired Rose's bicycle for nothing when he saw that it needed fixing. There were many good men, in fact, and perhaps there would be a good man in due course for Motholeli. It was possible.

That is, of course, if she wanted to find a husband. It was perfectly possible to be happy without a husband, or at least a bit happy. She herself was happy in her single state, but she thought, on balance, that it would be preferable to have a husband. She looked forward to the day when she would be able to make sure that Mr J.L.B. Matekoni was properly fed. She looked forward to the day when, if there was a noise in the night—as there often was these days—it would be Mr J.L.B.

Matekoni who would get up to investigate, rather than herself. We do need somebody else in this life, thought Mma Ramotswe; we need a person whom we can make our little god on this earth, as the old Kgatla saying had it. Whether it was a spouse, or a child, or a parent, or anybody else for that matter, there must be somebody who gives our lives purpose. She had always had the Daddy, the late Obed Ramotswe, miner, cattle farmer, and gentleman. It had given her pleasure to do things for him in his lifetime, and now it was a pleasure to do things for his memory. But the memory of a father went only so far.

Of course, there were those who said that none of this required marriage. They were right, to an extent. You did not have to be married to have somebody in your life, but then you would have no guarantee of permanence. Marriage itself did not offer that, but at least both people said that they wanted a lifelong union. Even if they proved to be wrong, at least they had tried. Mma Ramotswe had no time for those who decried marriage. In the old days, marriage had been a trap for women, because it gave men most of the rights and left women with the duties. Tribal marriage had been like that, although women acquired respect and status as they grew older, particularly if they were the mothers of sons. Mma Ramotswe did not support any of that, and thought that the modern notion of marriage, which was meant to be a union of equals, was a very different thing for a woman. Women had made a very bad mistake, she thought, in allowing themselves to be tricked into abandoning a belief in marriage. Some women thought that this would be a release from the tyranny of men, and in a way it had been that, but then it had also been a fine chance for men to behave selfishly. If you were a man and you were told that you could be with one woman until you got tired of her and then you could easily go on to a younger one, and all the time nobody would say that your behaviour was bad—because you were not committing adultery and so what wrong were you doing?—then that would suit you very well indeed.

"Who is doing all the suffering these days?" Mma Ramotswe had asked Mma Makutsi one day, as they sat in their office and waited for a client to appear. "Is it not women who have been left by their men going off with younger girls? Is that not what happens? A man gets to forty-five and decides that he has had enough. So he goes off with a younger woman."

"You are right, Mma," said Mma Makutsi. "It is the women of Botswana who are suffering, not the men. The men are very happy. I have seen it with my own eyes. I saw it at the Botswana Secretarial College."

Mma Ramotswe waited for more details.

"There were many glamorous girls at the College," went on Mma Makutsi. "These were the ones who did not do very well. They got fifty percent, or just over. They used to go out three or four nights a week, and many of them would meet older men, who would have more money and a nice car. These girls did not care that these men were married. They would go out with these men and dance in the bars. Then, what would happen, Mma?"

Mma Ramotswe shook her head. "I can imagine."

Mma Makutsi took off her glasses and polished them on her blouse. "They would tell these men to leave their wives. And the men would say that this was a good idea, and they would go off with these girls. And there would be many unhappy women who now would not be able to get another man because the men only go for young glamorous girls and they do not want an older woman. That is what I saw happening, Mma, and I could give you a list of names. A whole list."

"You do not need to," said Mma Ramotswe. "I have got a very long list of unhappy ladies. Very long."

"And how many unhappy men do you know?" went on Mma Makutsi. "How many men do you know who are sitting at home and thinking what to do now that their wife has gone off with a younger man? How many, Mma?"

"None," said Mma Ramotswe. "Not one."

"There you are," said Mma Makutsi. "Women have been tricked. They have tricked us, Mma. And we walked into their trap like cattle."

THE CHILDREN dispatched to school, Mma Ramotswe packed her small brown suitcase and began the drive out of town, out past the breweries and the new factories, the new low-cost suburb, with its rows of small, breeze-block houses, over the railway line which led to Francistown and Bulawayo, and onto the road that would lead her to the troubled place that was her destination. The first rains had come, and the parched brown veld was turning green, giving sweet grass to the cattle and the wandering herds of goats. The tiny white van had no radio—or no radio that worked—but Mma Ramotswe knew songs that she could sing, and she sang them, the window open, the crisp air of morning in her lungs, the birds flying up from the side of the road, plumage glistening; and above her, empty beyond emptiness, that sky that went on for miles and miles, the palest of blues.

She had felt uneasy about her mission, largely because what

she was about to do, she felt, was a breach of the fundamental principles of hospitality. You do not go into a house, as a guest, under false colours; and this was precisely what she was doing. Certainly, she was the guest of the father and mother, but even they did not know the true purpose of her visit. They were receiving her as one to whom their son owed a favour; whereas she was really a spy. She was a spy in a good cause, naturally, but that did not change the fact that her goal was to penetrate the family to find out a secret.

But now, in the tiny white van, she decided to put moral doubts aside. It was one of those situations where there were sound points to be made on both sides. She had decided that she would do it, because it was, on balance, better to act out a lie than to allow a life to be lost. Doubts should now be put away and the goal pursued wholeheartedly. There was no point in agonising over the decision you had made and wondering whether it was the right one. Besides, moral scruples would prevent the part from being played with conviction, and this might show. It would be like an actor questioning the part that he was playing mid-role.

She passed a man driving a mule cart, and waved. He took a hand from the rein and waved back, as did his passengers on the cart, two elderly women, a younger woman, and a child. They would be going out to the lands, thought Mma Ramotswe; a little bit late, perhaps, as they should have ploughed by the time that the first rains came, but they would sow their seed in time and they would have corn, and melons, and beans, perhaps by harvest time. There were several sacks on the cart, and these would contain the seed and the family's food, as well, while they were out on the lands. The women would make porridge and if the boys were lucky they might catch something for the pot—a guinea fowl would make a delicious stew for the whole family.

Mma Ramotswe saw the cart and the family retreating in the rearview mirror, as if they were going back into the past, getting smaller and smaller. One day people would no longer do this; they would no longer go out to the lands for the planting, and they would buy their food in stores, as people did in town. But what a loss for the country that would be; what friendship, and solidarity, and feeling for the land would be sacrificed if that were to happen. She had gone out to the lands as a girl, travelling with her aunts, and had stayed there while the boys had been sent to the cattle posts, where they would live for months in almost complete isolation, supervised by a few old men. She had loved the time at the lands, and had not been bored. They had swept the yards and woven grass; they had weeded the melon patches and told one another long stories about events that never happened, but could happen, perhaps, in another Botswana, somewhere else.

And then, when it had rained, they had cowered in the huts and heard the thunder roll above the land and smelled the lightning when it came too close, that acrid smell of burned air. When the rains had let up, they had gone outside and waited for the flying ants, which would emerge from their holes in the moistened ground and which could be picked up before they took flight, or plucked from the air as they began their journey, and eaten there and then, for the taste of butter.

She passed Pilane, and glanced down the road to Mochudi, to her right. This was a good place for her, and a bad one too. It was a good place, because it was the village of her girlhood; a bad place because right there, not far from the turnoff, was the place where a path crossed the railroad and her mother had died on that awful night, when the train had struck her. And although Precious Ramotswe was only a baby, that had been the shadow across her life; the mother whom she could not remember.

Now she was getting close to her destination. She had been given exact directions, and the gate was there, in the cattle fence, exactly where she had been told it would be. She drew off the road and got out to deal with the gate. Then, setting off on the dirt track that led west, she made her way to the small compound of houses that she could see about a mile or so distant, tucked amongst a cover of bush and overlooked by the tower of a metal windmill. This was a substantial farm, thought Mma Ramotswe, and she felt a momentary pang. Obed Ramotswe would have loved to have had a place like this, but although he had done well with his cattle, he had never been quite rich enough to have a large farm of this type. This would be six thousand acres, at least; maybe more.

The farm compound was dominated by a large, rambling house, topped by a red tin roof and surrounded on all sides by shady verandahs. This was the original farmhouse, and it had been encircled, over the years, by further buildings, two of which were houses themselves. The farmhouse was framed on either side by a luxuriant growth of purple-flowered bougainvillaea, and there were paw-paw trees behind it and to one side. An effort had been made to provide as much shade as possible—for not far to the west, perhaps just a bit farther than the eye could see, the land changed and the Kalahari began. But here, still, there was water, and the bush was good for cattle. Indeed, not too far to the east, the Limpopo began, not much of a river at that point, but capable of flowing in the rainy season.

There was a truck parked up against an outbuilding, and Mma Ramotswe left the tiny white van there. There was an enticing place under the shade of one of the largest trees, but it would have been rude of Mma Ramotswe to choose such a spot, which would be likely to be the parking place of a senior member of the family.

She left her suitcase on the passenger seat beside her and walked towards the gate that gave access to the front yard of the main house. She called out; it would have been discourteous to barge in without an invitation. There was no reply, and so she called out again. This time, a door opened and a middle-aged woman came out, drying her hands on her apron. She greeted Mma Ramotswe politely and invited her to come into the house.

"She is expecting you," she said. "I am the senior maid here. I look after the old woman. She has been waiting for you."

It was cool under the eaves of the verandah, and even cooler in the dim interior of the house. It took Mma Ramotswe's eyes a moment or two to get accustomed to the change in light, and at first there seemed to be more shadows that shapes; but then she saw the straight-backed chair on which the old woman was sitting, and the table beside her with the jug of water and the teapot.

They exchanged greetings, and Mma Ramotswe curtsied to the old woman. This pleased her hostess, who saw that here was a woman who understood the old ways, unlike those cheeky modern women from Gaborone who thought they knew everything and paid no attention to the elders. Ha! They thought they were clever; they thought they were this and that, doing men's jobs and behaving like female dogs when it came to men. Ha! But not here, out in the country, where the old ways still counted for something; and certainly not in this house.

"You are very kind to have me to stay here, Mma. Your son is a good man, too."

The old woman smiled. "No, Mma. That is all right. I am sorry to hear that you are having troubles in your life. These troubles that seem big, big in town are small troubles when you are out here. What matters out here? The rain. The grass for the cattle. None of the things that people are fretting over in town. They mean nothing when you are out here. You'll see."

"It is a nice place," said Mma Ramotswe. "It is very peaceful."

The old woman looked thoughtful. "Yes, it is peaceful. It has always been peaceful, and I would not want that to change." She poured out a glass of water and passed it to Mma Ramotswe.

"You should drink that, Mma. You must be very thirsty after your journey."

Mma Ramotswe took the glass, thanked her, and put it to her lips. As she did so, the old woman watched her carefully.

"Where are you from, Mma?" she said. "Have you always lived in Gaborone?"

Mma Ramotswe was not surprised by the question. This was a polite way of finding out where allegiances lay. There were eight main tribes in Botswana—and some smaller ones—and although most younger people did not think these things should be too important, for the older generation they counted a great deal. This woman, with her high status in tribal society, would be interested in these matters.

"I am from Mochudi," she said. "That is where I was born."

The old woman seemed visibly to relax. "Ah! So you are Kgatla, like us. Which ward did you live in?"

Mma Ramotswe explained her origins, and the old woman nodded. She knew that headman, yes, and she knew his cousin, who was married to her brother's wife's sister. Yes, she thought that she had met Obed Ramotswe a long time ago, and then, dredging into memory, she said, "Your mother is late, isn't she? She was the one who was killed by a train when you were a baby."

Mma Ramotswe was mildly surprised, but not astonished, that she should know this. There were people who made it their business to remember the affairs of the community, and this was obviously one. Today they called them oral historians, she believed; whereas in reality, they were old women who liked to remember the things that interested them most: marriages, deaths, children. Old men remembered cattle.

Their conversation went on, the old woman slowly and subtly extracting from Mma Ramotswe the full story of her life. She told her about Note Mokoti, and the old woman shook her head in sympathy, but said that there were many men like that and that women should look out for them.

"My family chose my husband for me," she said. "They started negotiations, although they would not have pressed the matter if I had said that I didn't like him. But they did the choosing and they knew what sort of man would be good for me. And they were right. My husband is a very fine husband, and I have given him three sons. There is one who is very interested in counting cattle, which is his hobby; he is a very clever man, in his way. Then there is the one you know, Mma, who is a very big man in the Government, and then there is the one who lives here. He is a very good farmer and has won prizes for his bulls. They are all fine men. I am proud."

"And have you been happy, Mma?" asked Mma Ramotswe. "Would you change your life at all if somebody came and said: here is some medicine to change your life. Would you do it?"

"Never," said the old woman. "Never. Never. God has given me everything a person could ask for. A good husband. Three strong sons. Strong legs that even today can take me walking five, six miles without any complaint. And you see here, look. All my teeth are still in my head. Seventy-six years and no teeth gone. My husband is the same. Our teeth will last until we are one hundred. Maybe longer."

"That is very lucky," said Mma Ramotswe. "Everything is very good for you."

"Almost everything," said the old woman.

Mma Ramotswe waited. Was she due to say something more? Perhaps she might reveal something she had seen her daughter-in-law do. Perhaps she had seen her preparing the poison, or had word of it somehow, but all she said was: "When the rains come, I find that my arms ache in the wet air. Here, and just here. For two months, three months, I have very sore arms that make it difficult to do any sewing. I have tried every medicine, but nothing works. So I think, if this is all that God has sent me to carry in this life, then I am still a very lucky woman."

THE MAID who had shown Mma Ramotswe in was summoned to take her to her room, which was at the back of the house. It was simply furnished, with a patchwork bedcover and a framed picture of Mochudi Hill on the wall. There was a table, with a crocheted white doily, and a small chest of drawers in which clothes could be stored.

"There is no curtain in this room," said the maid. "But nobody ever goes past this window and you will be private here, Mma."

She left Mma Ramotswe to unpack her clothes. There would be lunch at twelve o'clock, the maid explained, and until then she should entertain herself.

"There is nothing to do here," said the maid, adding, wistfully, "This is not Gaborone, you know."

The maid started to leave, but Mma Ramotswe prolonged the conversation. In her experience, the best way of getting somebody to talk was to get them to speak about themselves. This maid would have views, she felt; she was clearly not a stupid woman, and she spoke good, well-enunciated Setswana.

"Who else lives here, Mma?" she asked. "Are there other members of the family?"

"Yes," said the maid. "There are other people. There is their son and his wife. They have three sons, you see. One who has got a very small head and who counts cattle all day, all the time. He is always out at the cattle post and he never comes here. He is like a small boy, you see, and that is why he stays with the herdboys out there. They treat him like one of them, although he is a grown man. That is one. Then there is the one in Gaborone, where he is very important, and the one here. Those are the sons."

"And what do you think of those sons, Mma?"

It was a direct question and probably posed prematurely, which was risky; the woman could become suspicious at such prying. But she did not; instead she sat down on the bed.

"Let me tell you, Mma," she began. "That son who is out at

the cattle post is a very sad man. But you should hear the way that his mother talks about him. She says he is clever! Clever! Him! He is a little boy, Mma. It is not his fault, but that is what he is. The cattle post is the best place for him, but they should not say that he is clever. That is just a lie, Mma. It is like saying that there is rain in the dry season. There isn't."

"No," said Mma Ramotswe. "That is true."

The maid barely acknowledged her intervention before continuing. "And then that one in Gaborone; when he comes out here he makes trouble for everybody. He asks us all sorts of questions. He pokes his nose into everything. He even shouts at his father, would you believe it? But then the mother shouts at him and puts him in his place. He may be a big man in Gaborone, but here he is just the son and he should not shout at his elders."

Mma Ramotswe was delighted. This was exactly the sort of maid she liked to interview.

"You are right, Mma," she said. "There are too many people shouting at other people these days. Shout. Shout. You hear it all the time. But why do you think he shouts? Is it just to clear his voice?"

The maid laughed. "He has a big voice, that one! No, he shouts because he says that there is something wrong in this place. He says that things are not being done properly. And then he says . . ." She lowered her voice. "And then he says that the wife of his brother is a bad woman. He said that to the father, in so many words. I heard him. People think that maids don't hear, but we have ears the same as anybody. I heard him say that. He said wicked things about her."

Mma Ramotswe raised an eyebrow. "Wicked things?"

"He says that she is sleeping with other men. He says that

when they have their firstborn it will not be of this house. He says that their sons will belong to other men and different blood will get this farm. That's what he says."

Mma Ramotswe was silent. She looked out of her window. There was bougainvillaea directly outside, and its shadow was purple. Beyond it, the tops of the thorn trees, stretching out to the low hills on the horizon; a lonely land, at the beginning of the emptiness.

"And do you think that's true, Mma? Is there any truth in what he says about that woman?"

The maid crumpled up her features. "Truth, Mma? Truth? That man does not know what truth means. Of course it is not true. That woman is a good woman. She is the cousin of my mother's cousin. All the family, all of them, are Christians. They read the Bible. They follow the Lord. They do not sleep with other men. That is one thing which is true."

CHAPTER THIRTEEN

THE CHIEF JUSTICE OF BEAUTY

MMA MAKUTSI, Acting Manager of Tlokweng Road Speedy Motors and assistant detective at the No. 1 Ladies' Detective Agency, went to work that day in some trepidation. Although she welcomed responsibility and had delighted in her two promotions, she had nonetheless always had Mma Ramotswe in the background, a presence to whom she could turn if she found herself out of her depth. Now, with Mma Ramotswe away, she realised that she was solely responsible for two businesses and two employees. Even if Mma Ramotswe was planning to be no more than four or five days on the farm, that was long enough for things to go wrong and, since Mma Ramotswe could not be contacted by telephone, Mma Makutsi would have to handle everything. As far as the garage was concerned, she knew that Mr J.L.B. Matekoni was now being looked after at the orphan farm and that she should not attempt to contact him until he was better. Rest and a complete break from the worries of work had been advised by the doctor, and Mma Potokwane, not accustomed to contradicting doctors, would be fiercely protective of her patient.

Mma Makutsi secretly hoped that the agency would get no clients until Mma Ramotswe came back. This was not because she did not want to work on a case—she certainly did—but she did not wish to be solely and completely responsible. But, of course, a client did come in, and, what was worse, it was a client with a problem that required immediate attention.

Mma Makutsi was sitting at Mr J.L.B. Matekoni's desk, preparing garage bills, when one of the apprentices put his head round the door.

"There is a very smart-looking man wanting to see you, Mma," he announced, wiping his greasy hands on his overalls. "I have opened the agency door and told him to wait."

Mma Makutsi frowned at the apprentice. "Smart-looking?"

"Big suit," said the apprentice. "You know. Handsome, same as me but not quite. Shiny shoes. A very smart man. You watch yourself, Mma. Men like that try to charm ladies like you. You just see."

"Don't wipe your hands on your overalls," snapped Mma Makutsi, as she rose from her chair. "We pay for the laundering. You don't. We give you cotton waste to use for that purpose. That is what it's for. Has Mr J.L.B. Matekoni not told you that?"

"Maybe," said the apprentice. "Maybe not. The boss said lots of things to us. We can't remember everything he says."

Mma Makutsi brushed past him on her way out. These boys are impossible, she thought, but at least they were proving to be harder workers than she expected. Perhaps Mr J.L.B. Matekoni had been too soft on them in the past; he was such a kind man and it was not in his nature to criticise people unduly. Well, it was in her nature at least. She was a graduate of the Botswana Secretarial College, and the College teachers had always said: Do not be afraid to criticize—in a constructive way, of course—your own performance and, if necessary, the performance of others. Well, Mma Makutsi had criticised, and it had borne fruit. The garage was doing well and there seemed to be more and more work each day.

She paused at the door of the agency, just round the corner of the building, and looked at the car parked under the tree behind her. This man—this smart man, as the apprentice had described him—certainly drove an attractive car. She ran her eye for a moment over the smooth lines of the vehicle and its double aerials, front and back. Why would somebody need so many aerials? It would be impossible to listen to more than one radio station at a time, or make more than one telephone call while driving. But whatever the explanation, they certainly added to the air of glamour and importance which surrounded the car.

She pushed the door open. Inside, seated in the chair facing Mma Ramotswe's desk, knees crossed in relaxed elegance, was Mr Moemedi "Two Shots" Pulani, immediately recognisable to any reader of the *Botswana Daily News,* across whose columns his handsome, self-assured face had so often been printed. Mma Makutsi's immediate thought was that the apprentice should have recognised him, and she felt momentarily annoyed at his failure to do so, but then she reminded herself that the apprentice was an apprentice mechanic and not an apprentice detective, and, furthermore, she had never seen the apprentices reading the newspapers anyway. They read a South African motorcycle magazine, which they pored over in fascination, and a publication called *Fancy Girls* which they attempted to hide from Mma Makutsi whenever she came across them peering at it during their lunch hour. So there was no reason, she realised, for them to know about Mr Pulani, his fashion empire, and his well-known work for local charities.

Mr Pulani rose to his feet as she entered and greeted her politely. They shook hands, and then Mma Makutsi walked round the desk and sat in Mma Ramotswe's chair.

"I am glad that you could see me without an appointment, Mma Ramotswe," said Mr Pulani, taking a silver cigarette case out of his breast pocket.

"I am not Mma Ramotswe, Rra," she said, declining his offer of a cigarette. "I am the Assistant Manager of the agency." She paused. It was not strictly true that she was the Assistant Manager of the agency; in fact, it was quite untrue. But she was certainly managing it in Mma Ramotswe's absence, and so perhaps the description was justified.

"Ah," said Mr Pulani, lighting his cigarette with a large gold-plated lighter. "I would like to speak to Mma Ramotswe herself, please."

Mma Makutsi flinched as the cloud of smoke drifted over the table to her.

"I'm sorry," she said. "That will not be possible for some days. Mma Ramotswe is investigating a very important case abroad." She paused again. The exaggeration had come so easily, and without any thought. It sounded more impressive that Mma Ramotswe should be abroad—it gave the agency an international feel—but she should not have said it.

"I see," said Mr Pulani. "Well, Mma, in that case I shall speak to you."

"I am listening, Rra."

Mr Pulani leaned back in his seat. "This is very urgent. Will you be able to look into something today, straightaway?"

Mma Makutsi took a deep breath before the next cloud of smoke engulfed her.

"We are at your disposal," she said. "Of course, it is more expensive to handle things urgently. You'll understand that, Rra."

He brushed her warning aside. "Expense is not the issue," he said. "What is at issue is the whole future of the Miss Beauty and Integrity contest."

He paused for the effect of his words to be felt. Mma Makutsi obliged.

"Oh! That is a very serious matter."

Mr Pulani nodded. "Indeed it is, Mma. And we have three days to deal with this issue. Just three days."

"Tell me about it, Rra. I am ready to listen."

"THERE IS an interesting background to this, Mma," began Mr Pulani. "I think that the story begins a long time ago, a long time. In fact, the story begins in the Garden of Eden, when God made Adam and Eve. You will remember that Eve tempted Adam because she was so beautiful. And women have continued to be beautiful in the eyes of men since that time, and they still are, as you know.

"Now, the men of Botswana like pretty ladies. They are always looking at them, even when they are elders, and thinking that is a pretty woman, or that this woman is prettier than that woman, and so on."

"They are like that with cattle, too," interjected Mma Makutsi. "They say this cow is a good cow and this one is not so good. Cattle. Women. It's all the same to men."

Mr Pulani cast her a sideways glance. "Maybe. That is one way of looking at it. Perhaps." He paused briefly before continuing. "Anyway, it is this interest of men in pretty ladies that makes beauty competitions so popular here in Botswana. We like to find the most beautiful ladies in Botswana and give them titles and prizes. It is a very important form of entertainment for men. And I am one such man, Mma. I have been involved in the beauty queen world for fifteen years, nonstop. I am maybe the most important person in the beauty side of things."

"I have seen your picture in the papers, Rra," said Mma Makutsi. "I have seen you presenting prizes."

Mr Pulani nodded. "I started the Miss Glamorous Botswana competition five years ago, and now it is the top one. The lady who wins our competition always gets into the Miss Botswana competition and sometimes into the Miss Universe competition. We have sent ladies to New York and Palm Springs; they have been given high marks for beauty. Some say that they are our best export after diamonds."

"And cattle," added Mma Makutsi.

"Yes, and cattle," Mr Pulani agreed. "But there are some people who are always sniping at us. They write to the newspapers and tell us that it is wrong to encourage ladies to dress up and walk in front of a lot of men like that. They say that it encourages false values. Pah! False values? These people who write these letters are just jealous. They are envious of the beauty of these girls. They know that they would never be able to enter a competition like that. So they complain and complain and they are very happy when something goes wrong for a beauty competition. They forget, by the way, that these competitions raise a lot of money for charity. Last year, Mma, we raised five thousand pula for the hospital, twenty thousand pula for drought relief—twenty thousand, Mma—and almost eight thousand pula for a nursing scholarship fund. Those are big sums, Mma. How much money have our critics raised? I can tell you the answer to that. Nothing.

"But we have to be careful. We get a lot of money from sponsors, and if sponsors withdraw, then we are in trouble. So if something goes wrong for our competition, then the sponsors may say that they do not want to have anything more to do with us. They say that they do not want to be embarrassed by bad publicity. They say that they are paying for good publicity, not for bad."

"And has something gone wrong?"

Mr Pulani tapped his fingers on the desk. "Yes. Some very bad things have happened. Last year, two of our beauty queens were found to be bad girls. One was arrested for prostitution in one of the big hotels. That was not good. Another was shown to have obtained goods under false pretences and to have used a credit card without authorisation. There were letters in the paper. There was much crowing. They said things like: Are these girls the right sort of girls to be ambassadors for Botswana? Why not go straight to the prison and pick some of the women prisoners and make them beauty queens? They thought that was very funny, but it was not. Some of the companies saw this and said that if this happened again, they would withdraw sponsorship. I had four letters, all saying the same thing.

"So I decided that this year the theme of our competition would be Beauty and Integrity. I told our people that we must choose beauty queens who are good citizens, who will not embarrass us in this way. It is the only way that we are going to keep our sponsors happy.

"So for the first round, all the ladies had to fill in a form which I designed myself. This asked all sorts of questions about their views. It asked things like: Would you like to work for charity? Then it asked: What are the values which a good citizen of Botswana should uphold? And: Is it better to give than receive?

"All the girls filled in these questions, and only those who showed that they understood the meaning of good citizenship were allowed to go on to the finals. From these girls we made a shortlist of five. I went to the papers and told them that we had found five very good citizens who believed in the best values. There was an article in the *Botswana Daily News* which said: *Good girls seek beauty title.*

"I was very happy, and there was silence from our critics, who had to sit on their hands because they could not come out and criticise these ladies who wanted to be good citizens. The sponsors telephoned me and said that they were content to be identified with the values of good citizenship and that if all went well they would continue to provide their sponsorship next year. And the charities themselves said to me that this was the way of the future."

Mr Pulani paused. He looked at Mma Makutsi, and for a moment his urbane manner deserted him and he looked crestfallen. "Then, yesterday I heard the bad news. One of our short-listed girls was arrested by the police and charged with shoplifting. I heard about it through one of my employees and when I checked with a friend who is an inspector of police, he said that it was true. This girl had been found shoplifting in the Game store. She tried to steal a large cooking pot by slipping it under her blouse. But she did not notice that the handle was sticking out of the side and the store detective stopped her. Fortunately it has not got into the newspapers, and with any luck it will not, at least until the case comes up in the Magistrate's Court."

Mma Makutsi felt a pang of sympathy for Mr Pulani. In spite of his flashiness, there was no doubt that he did a great deal for charity. The fashion world was inevitably flashy, and he was probably no worse than any of the others, but at least he was doing his best for people in trouble. And beauty competitions were a fact of life, which you could not wish out of existence. If he was trying to make his competition more acceptable, then he deserved support.

"I am sorry to hear that, Rra," she said. "That must have been very bad news for you."

"Yes," he said, miserably. "And it is made much worse by the fact that the finals are in three days. There are now only four girls on the list, but how do I know that they are not going to embarrass me? That one must have lied when she filled in her questionnaire and made out that she was a good citizen. How do I know that the rest of them aren't lying when they say that they would like to do things for charity? How do I know that? And if we choose a girl who is a liar, then she may well prove to be a thief or whatever. And that means that we are bound to face embarrassment once she gets going."

Mma Makutsi nodded. "It is very difficult. You really need to be able to look into the hearts of the remaining four. If there is a good one there . . ."

"If there is such a lady," said Mr Pulani forcefully, "then she will win. I can arrange for her to win."

"But what about the other judges?" asked Mma Makutsi.

"I am the chief judge," he said. "You might call me the Chief Justice of Beauty. My vote is the one that counts."

"I see."

"Yes. That is the way it works."

Mr Pulani stubbed out his cigarette on the sole of his shoe. "So you see, Mma. That is what I want you to do. I will give you the names and addresses of the four ladies. I would like you to find out if there is one really good lady there. If you can't find that, then at least tell me which is the most honest of the lot. That would be second best."

Mma Makutsi laughed. "How can I look into the hearts of these girls that quickly?" she asked. "I would have to talk to many, many people to find out about them. It could take weeks."

Mr Pulani shrugged. "You haven't got weeks, Mma. You've got three days. You did say that you could help me."

"Yes, but . . ."

Mr Pulani reached into a pocket and took out a piece of paper. "This is a list of the four names. I have written the address of each lady after her name. They all live in Gaborone." He slipped the piece of paper across the desk and then extracted a thin leather folder from another pocket. As he opened it, Mma Makutsi saw that it contained a chequebook. He opened it and began to write. "And here, Mma, is a cheque for two thousand pula, made payable to the No. 1 Ladies' Detective Agency. There. It's postdated. If you can give me the information I need the day after tomorrow, you can present this at the bank the next day."

Mma Makutsi stared at the cheque. She imagined how it would feel to be able to say to Mma Ramotswe when she returned, "I earned the agency two thousand pula in fees, Mma, already paid." She knew that Mma Ramotswe was not a greedy woman, but she also knew that she worried about the financial viability of the agency. A fee of that size would help a great deal, and would be a reward, thought Mma Makutsi, for the confidence that Mma Ramotswe had shown in her.

She slipped the cheque into a drawer. As she did so, she saw Mr Pulani relax.

"I am counting on you, Mma," he said. "Everything that I have heard about the No. 1 Ladies' Detective Agency has been good. I hope that I shall see that for myself."

"I hope so too, Rra," said Mma Makutsi. But she was already feeling doubtful about how she could possibly find out which of the four short-listed ladies were honest. It seemed an impossible task.

She escorted Mr Pulani to the door, noticing for the first time that he was wearing white shoes. She observed, too, his large gold cuff links and his tie with its sheen of silk. She would not like to have a man like that, she thought. One would have to spend all one's time at a beauty parlour in order to keep up the appearance he would no doubt expect. Of course, reflected Mma Makutsi, that would suit some ladies perfectly well.

CHAPTER FOURTEEN

GOD DECIDED THAT BOTSWANA WOULD BE A DRY PLACE

THE MAID had said that the midday meal would be at one o'clock, which was several hours away. Mma Ramotswe decided that the best way of spending this time would be to familiarise herself with her surroundings. She liked farms—as most Batswana did—because they reminded her of her childhood and of the true values of her people. They shared the land with cattle, and with birds and the many other creatures that could be seen if one only watched. It was easy perhaps not to think about this in the town, where there was food to be had from shops and where running water came from taps, but for many people this was not how life was.

After her revealing conversation with the maid, she left her room and made her way out of the front door. The sun was hot overhead, and shadows were short. To the east, over the low, distant hills, blue under their heat haze, heavy rain clouds were building up. There could be rain later on if the clouds built up further, or at least there would be rain for somebody, out there, along the border. It looked as if the rains would be good this year, which is what everybody was praying for. Good rains meant full stomachs; drought meant thin cattle and wilted crops. They had experienced a bad drought a few years previously, and the Government, its heart heavy, had instructed people to start slaughtering their cattle. That was the worst thing for anybody to have to do, and the suffering had cut deep.

Mma Ramotswe looked about her. There was a paddock some distance off, and cattle were crowded around a drinking trough. A pipe ran from the creaking windmill and its concrete storage tank over the surface of the ground to the trough and the thirsty cattle. Mma Ramotswe decided that she would go and take a look at the cattle. She was, after all, the daughter of Obed Ramotswe, whose eye for cattle was said by many to have been one of the best in Botswana. She could tell a good beast when she saw one, and sometimes, when she drove past a particularly handsome specimen on the road, she would think of what the Daddy would have said about it. Good shoulders, perhaps; or, that is a good cow; look at the way she is walking; or, that bull is all talk, I do not think that he would make many calves.

This farm would have a large number of cattle, perhaps five or six thousand. For most people, that was riches beyond dreaming; ten or twenty cattle were quite enough to make one feel that one had at least some wealth, and she would be happy with that. Obed Ramotswe had built up his herd by judicious buying and selling and had ended up with two thousand cattle at the end of his life. It was this that had provided her with her legacy and with the means to buy the house in Zebra Drive and start the agency. And there were cattle left over, some which she had decided not to sell and which were looked after by herdboys at a distant cattle post which a cousin visited for her. There were sixty of them, she thought; all fine descendants of the lumbering Brahman bulls which her father had so painstakingly selected and bred. One day she would go out there, travelling on the ox-wagon, and see them; it would be an emotional occasion, because they were a link with the Daddy and she would miss him acutely, she knew, and she would probably weep and they would wonder why this woman still wept for her father who had died long ago now.

We still have tears to shed, she thought. We still have to weep for those mornings when we went out early and watched the cows amble along the cattle paths and the birds flying high in the thermal currents.

"What are you thinking of, Mma?"

She looked up. A man had appeared beside her, a stock whip in his hand, a battered hat on his head.

Mma Ramotswe greeted him. "I am thinking of my late father," she said. "He would have liked to see these cattle here. Do you look after them, Rra? They are fine beasts."

He smiled in appreciation. "I have looked after these cattle all their lives. They are like my children. I have two hundred children, Mma. All cattle."

Mma Ramotswe laughed. "You must be a busy man, Rra."

He nodded, and took a small paper packet out of his pocket. He offered Mma Ramotswe a piece of dried beef, which she accepted.

"You are staying at the house?" he asked. "They often have people coming up here and staying. Sometimes the son who is in Gaborone brings his friends from the Government. I have seen them with my own eyes. Those people."

"He is very busy that one," said Mma Ramotswe. "Do you know him well?"

"Yes," said the man, chewing on a piece of beef. "He comes out here and tells us what to do. He worries about the cattle all the time. He says this one is sick, that one is lame. Where is that other one? All the time. Then he goes away and things get back to normal."

Mma Ramotswe frowned sympathetically. "That cannot be easy for his brother, the other one, can it?"

The cattleman opened his eyes wide. "He stands there like a dog and lets his brother shout at him. He is a good farmer, that younger one, but the firstborn still thinks that he is the one who is running this farm. But we know that their father had spoken to the chief and it had been agreed that the younger one would get most of the cattle and the older one could have money. That is what was decided."

"But the older one doesn't like it?"

"No," said the cattleman. "And I suppose I can see how he feels. But he has done very well in Gaborone and he has another life. The younger one is the farmer. He knows cattle."

"And what about the third one?" asked Mma Ramotswe. "The one who is out that way?" She pointed towards the Kalahari.

The cattleman laughed. "He is just a boy. It is very sad. There is air in his head, they say. It is because of something that the mother did when he was in her womb. That is how these things happen."

"Oh?" said Mma Ramotswe. "What did she do?" She knew of the belief which people in the country had that a handicapped child was the result of some bad act on the parents' part. If a woman had an affair with another man, for example, then that could lead to the birth of a simpleton. If a man rejected his wife and went off with another woman while she was expecting his child, that, too, could lead to disaster for the baby.

The cattleman lowered his voice. But who was there to hear, thought Mma Ramotswe, but the cattle and the birds?

"She is the one to watch," said the man. "She is the one. The old woman. She is a wicked woman."

"Wicked?"

He nodded. "Watch her," he said. "Watch her eyes."

THE MAID came to her door shortly before two o'clock and told her that the meal was ready.

"They are eating in the porch on that side," she said, pointing to the other side of the house.

Mma Ramotswe thanked her and left her room. The porch was on the cooler side of the house, shaded by an awning of netting and a profusion of creepers that had been trained across a rough wooden trellis. Two tables had been drawn up alongside one another and covered with a starched white tablecloth. At one end of the large table, several dishes of food had been placed in a circle: steaming pumpkin, a bowl of maize meal, a plate of beans and other greens, and a large tureen of heavy meat stew. Then there was a loaf of bread and a dish of butter. It was good food, of the type which only a wealthy family could afford every day.

Mma Ramotswe recognised the old woman, who was sitting slightly back from the table, a small gingham cloth spread over her lap, but other members of the family were there too:

a child of about twelve, a young woman in a smart green skirt and a white blouse—the wife, Mma Ramotswe assumed—and a man at her side, dressed in long khaki trousers and a short-sleeved khaki shirt. The man stood up when Mma Ramotswe appeared and came out from behind the table to welcome her.

"You are our guest," he said, smiling as he spoke. "You are very welcome in this house, Mma."

The old woman nodded at her. "This is my son," she said. "He was with the cattle when you arrived."

The man introduced her to his wife, who smiled at her in a friendly way.

"It is very hot today, Mma," said the young woman. "But it is going to rain, I think. You have brought us this rain, I think."

It was a compliment, and Mma Ramotswe acknowledged it. "I hope so," she said. "The land is still thirsty."

"It is always thirsty," said the husband. "God decided that Botswana would be a dry place for dry animals. That is what he decided."

Mma Ramotswe sat down between the wife and the old woman. While the wife started to serve the meal, the husband poured water into the glasses.

"I saw you looking at the cattle," said the old woman. "Do you like cattle, Mma?"

"What Motswana does not like cattle?" replied Mma Ramotswe.

"Perhaps there are some," said the old woman. "Perhaps there are some who do not understand cattle. I don't know."

She turned away as she gave her answer and was now looking out through the tall, unglazed windows of the porch, out across the expanse of bush that ran away to the horizon.

"They tell me that you are from Mochudi," said the young woman, handing Mma Ramotswe her plate. "I am from there, too."

"That was some time ago," said Mma Ramotswe. "I am in Gaborone now. Like so many people."

"Like my brother," said the husband. "You must know him well if he is sending you out here."

There was a moment of silence. The old woman turned to look at her son, who looked away from her.

"I do not know him well," said Mma Ramotswe. "But he invited me to this house as a favour. I had helped him."

"You are very welcome," said the old woman quickly. "You are our guest."

The last remark was aimed at her son, but he was busy with his plate and affected not to notice what his mother had said. The wife, though, had caught Mma Ramotswe's eye when this exchange took place, and had then quickly looked away again.

They ate in silence. The old woman had her plate on her lap, and was busy excavating a pile of maize meal soaked in gravy. She placed the mixture in her mouth and chewed slowly on it, her rheumy eyes fixed on the view of the bush and the sky. For her part, the wife had helped herself only to beans and pumpkin, which she picked at halfheartedly. Looking down at her plate, Mma Ramotswe noticed that she and the husband were the only people who were eating stew. The child, who had been introduced as a cousin of the wife's, was eating a thick slice of bread onto which syrup and gravy had been ladled.

Mma Ramotswe looked at her food. She sank her fork into the pile of stew which nestled between a large helping of pumpkin and a small mound of maize meal. The stew was thick and glutinous, and when she took up her fork it trailed a thin trail of glycerine-like substance across the plate. But when she put the fork into her mouth, the food tasted normal, or almost normal. There was slight flavour, she thought, a flavour which she might have described as metallic, like the taste of the iron pills which her doctor had once given her, or perhaps bitter, like the taste of a split lemon pip.

She looked at the wife, who smiled at her.

"I am not the cook," the young woman said. "If this food tastes good, it is not because I cooked it. There is Samuel in the kitchen. He is a very good cook, and we are proud of him. He is trained. He is a chef."

"It is woman's work," said the husband. "That is why you do not find me in the kitchen. A man should be doing other things."

He looked at Mma Ramotswe as he spoke, and she sensed the challenge.

She took a moment or two to answer. Then: "That is what many people say, Rra. Or at least, that is what many men say. I am not sure whether many women say it, though."

The husband put down his fork. "You ask my wife," he said, quietly. "You ask her whether she says it. Go on."

The wife did not hesitate. "What my husband says is right," she said.

The old woman turned to Mma Ramotswe. "You see?" she said. "She supports her husband. That is how it is here in the country. In the town it may be different, but in the country that is how it is."

SHE RETURNED to her room after the meal and lay down on her bed. The heat had got no better, although the clouds had continued to build up in the east. It was clear now that there was going to be rain, even if it would not come until nighttime. There would be a wind soon, and with it would come that wonderful, unmistakable smell of rain, that smell of dust and water meeting that lingered for a few seconds in the nostrils and then was gone, and would be missed, sometimes for months, before the next time that it caught you and made you stop and say to the person with you, any person: That is the smell of rain, there, right now.

She lay on her bed and stared up at the white ceiling boards. They had been well dusted, which was a sign of good housekeeping. In many houses, the ceilings were fly-spotted or marked, at the edges, with the foundations of termite trails. Sometimes large spiders could be seen looping across what must have seemed to them upside-down white tundras. But here, there was nothing, and the paintwork was unsullied.

Mma Ramotswe was puzzled. All that she had learned today was that the staff had views, but that they all disliked the Government Man. He threw his weight around, it seemed, but was there anything untoward in that? Of course the older brother would have views on how the cattle should be handled, and of course it was natural for him to give these views to his younger brother. Of course the old woman would think that her handicapped son was clever; and of course she would believe that city people lost interest in cattle. Mma Ramotswe realised that she knew very little about her. The cattleman thought she was wicked, but he gave no reason to back up his assessment. He had told her to watch her eyes, which she had done, to no effect. All that she had noticed was that she looked away, into the distance, while they all had lunch together. What did this mean?

Mma Ramotswe sat up. There was something to be learned there, she thought. If somebody looked away, into the distance, then it meant that he or she did not want to be there. And the most common reason for not wanting to be somewhere was because one did not like the company one was in. That was always true. Now, if she was always looking away, that meant that she did not like somebody there. She does not dislike me, thought Mma Ramotswe, because she gave no indication of this when I saw her earlier and she has not had the chance to develop a dislike. The child would hardly have given rise to that sort of reaction, and indeed she had treated him quite fondly, patting his head on one or two occasions during the meal. That left the son and his wife.

No mother dislikes her son. Mma Ramotswe understood that there were women who were ashamed of their sons, and there were also women who were angry with their sons. But no mother actually disliked a son at heart. A son could do anything, and would be forgiven by his mother. This old woman, therefore, disliked her daughter-in-law and disliked her intensely enough to want to be somewhere else when she was in her company.

Mma Ramotswe lay back on her bed, the immediate excitement of her conclusion having passed. Now she had to establish why the old woman disliked the daughter-in-law, and if it was because her other son, the Government Man, had said something to her about his suspicions. Perhaps more important, though, was the question of whether the woman knew that her mother-in-law disliked her. If she did, then she would have a motive for doing something about it, but if she were a poisoner—and she did not look like it, and there were also the contrary views of the maid to be taken into account—then surely she would have attempted to poison the old woman rather than her husband.

Mma Ramotswe felt drowsy. She had not slept well the previous evening, and the drive and the heat and the heavy lunch were having their effect. The stew had been very rich; rich and viscous, with that glutinous trail. She closed her eyes, but did not see darkness. There was a white aura, a faint luminous line, that seemed to cross her inner vision. The bed moved slightly, as if with the wind that had now started to blow from over the border, far away. The rain smell came, and then the hot, urgent drops, punishing the ground, stinging it, and bouncing back up like tiny grey worms.

Mma Ramotswe slept, but her breathing was shallow, and her dreams were fevered. When she awoke and felt the pain in her stomach, it was almost five o'clock. The main storm had passed, but there was still rain, beating on the tin roof of the house like a troop of insistent drummers. She sat up, and then lay down again from the nausea. She turned on the bed and dropped her feet to the floor. Then she rose, unsteadily, and stumbled on her way to the door and the bathroom at the end of the corridor outside. There she was sick, and almost immediately felt better. By the time she had reached her room, the worst of the nausea had passed and she was able to reflect on her situation. She had come to the home of a poisoner and had been poisoned herself. She should not be surprised at that. Indeed it was entirely and completely predictable.

CHAPTER FIFTEEN

WHAT DO YOU WANT TO DO WITH YOUR LIFE?

MMA MAKUTSI had only three days. It was not a long time, and she wondered whether she could possibly find out enough about each of the four finalists to enable her to advise Mr Pulani. She looked at the neatly typed list which he had provided, but neither the names, nor the addresses which followed them, told her anything. She knew that there were people who claimed that they could judge people on their names, that girls called Mary were inevitably honest and home-loving, that you should never trust a Sipho, and so on. But this was an absurd notion, very much less helpful than the notion that you could tell whether a person was a criminal by looking at the shape of his head. Mma Ramotswe had shown her an article about that theory and she had joined her in her laughter. But the idea—even if clearly not a very appropriate one for a modern person like herself to hold—had intrigued her and she had discreetly embarked on her own researches.

The ever-helpful librarian of the British Council Library had produced a book within minutes and had pressed it into her hands. *Theories of Crime* was a considerably more scholarly work than Mma Ramotswe's professional bible, *The Principles of Private Detection* by Clovis Andersen. That was perfectly adequate for tips on dealing with clients, but it was weak on theory. It was obvious to Mma Makutsi that Clovis Andersen was no reader of *The Journal of Criminology;* whereas the author of *Theories of Crime* was quite familiar with the debates which took place as to what caused crime. Society was one possible culprit, Mma Makutsi read; bad housing and a bleak future made criminals of young men, and we should remember, the book warned, that those to whom evil was done *did evil in return.*

Mma Makutsi read this with astonishment. It was absolutely correct, she reflected, but she had never thought about it in those terms. Of course those who did wrong had been wronged themselves—that very much accorded with her own experience. In her third year at school, all those years ago in Bobonong, she remembered a boy who had bullied the smaller boys and had delighted in their terror. She had never been able to understand why he had done it—perhaps he was just evil—but then, one evening, she had passed by his house and had seen him being beaten by his drunken father. The boy wriggled and cried out, but had been unable to escape the blows. The following day, on the way to school, she had seen him striking a smaller boy and push him into a painful wagenbikkie bush with its cruel thorns. Of course she had not linked cause and effect at that age, but now it came back to her and she reflected on the wisdom revealed in the text of *Theories of Crime.*

Sitting alone in the office of the No. 1 Ladies' Detective Agency, it took her several hours of reading to reach what she was looking for. The section on biological explanations of crime was shorter than the other sections, largely because the author was clearly uncomfortable with them.

"The nineteenth century Italian criminologist, Cesare Lombroso," she read, "although liberal in his views of prison reform, was convinced that criminality could be detected by the shape of the head. Thus he expended a great deal of energy on charting the physiognomy of criminals, in a misguided attempt to identify those facial and cranial features that were indicative of criminality. These quaint illustrations (reproduced below) are a testament to the misplaced enthusiasm which could so easily have been directed into more fruitful lines of research."

Mma Makutsi looked at the illustrations taken from Lombroso's book. An evil-looking man with a narrow forehead and fiery eyes looked out at the reader. Underneath this picture was the legend: *Typical murderer* (*Sicilian type*). Then there was a picture of another man, elaborately moustachioed but with narrow, pinched eyes. This, she read, was a *Classic thief* (*Neapolitan type*). Other criminal "types" stared out at the reader, all of them quite unambiguously malign. Mma Makutsi gave a shudder. These were clearly extremely unpleasant men and nobody would trust any of them. Why, then, describe the theories of Lombroso as "misguided"? Not only was that rude, in her opinion, but it was patently wrong. Lombroso was right; you *could* tell (something which women had known for a very long time—they could tell what men were like just by looking at them, but they did not need to be Italian to do so; they could do it right here in Botswana). She was puzzled; if the theory was so clearly right, then why should the author of this criminological work deny it? She thought for a moment and then the explanation came to her: he was *jealous!* That must be the reason. He was jealous because Lombroso had thought about this before he had and he wanted to develop his own ideas about crime. Well! If that were the case, then she would bother no more with *Theories of Crime*. She had found out a bit more about this sort of criminology, and now all she had to do was apply it. She would use the theories of Lombrosan criminology to detect who, of the four girls on the list, was trustworthy and who was not. Lombroso's illustration had simply confirmed that she should trust her intuition. A brief time with these girls, and perhaps a discreet inspection of their cranial structures—she would not want to stare—would be enough to provide her with an answer. It would have to suffice; there was nothing else that she could do in the short time available and she was particularly keen that the matter should be satisfactorily resolved by the time of Mma Ramotswe's return.

FOUR NAMES, none of them known to Mma Makutsi: Motlamedi Matluli, Gladys Tlhapi, Makita Phenyonini, and Patricia Quatleneni; and beneath them, their ages and their addresses. Motlamedi was the youngest, at nineteen, and the most readily accessible—she was a student at the university. Patricia was the oldest at twenty-four, and possibly the most difficult to contact, at her vague address in Tlokweng (plot 2456). Mma Makutsi decided that she would visit Motlamedi first, as it would be a simple matter to find her in her students' hall on the neatly laid-out university campus. Of course, it would not necessarily be easy to interview her; Mma Makutsi knew that girls like that, with their place at the university and a good job virtually guaranteed for them, tended to look down on people who had not had their advantages, particularly those who had attended the Botswana Secretarial College. Her own 97 percent in the final examinations, the result of such hard work, would be mocked by one such as Motlamedi. But she would speak to her and treat any condescension with dignity. She had nothing to be ashamed of; she was now the Acting Manager of a garage, was she not, and an assistant detective as well. What official titles did this beautiful girl have? She was not even Miss Beauty and Integrity, even if she was in the running for that particular honour.

She would go to see her. But what would she say? She could hardly seek out this girl and then say to her: Excuse me, *I have come to look at your head.* That would invite a hostile response, even if it had the merits of being completely true. And then the idea came to her. She could pretend to be doing a survey of some sort, and while the girls were answering, she could look closely at their head and facial features to see if any of the telltale signs of dishonesty was present. And the idea became even better. The survey need not be some meaningless marketing survey of the sort which people were used to responding to; it could be a survey of moral attitudes. It could pose certain questions which, in a very subtle way, would uncover the girls' attitudes. The questions would be carefully phrased, so that the girls would not suspect a trap, but they would be as revealing as searchlights. *What do you really want to do with your life?* for example. Or: *Is it better to make a lot of money than to help others?*

The ideas fell neatly into place, and Mma Makutsi smiled

with delight as each new possibility revealed itself to her. She would claim to be a journalist, sent by the *Botswana Daily News* to write a feature article on the competition—small deceptions are permissible, Clovis Andersen had written, provided that the ends justified the means. Well, the ends in this case were clearly important, as the reputation of Botswana itself could be in the balance. The girl who won Miss Beauty and Integrity could find herself in the running for the title of Miss Botswana, and that post was every bit as important as being an ambassador. Indeed, a beauty queen was a sort of ambassador for her country, and people would judge the country on how she conducted herself. If she had to tell a small lie in order to prevent a wicked girl from seizing the title and bringing shame to the country, then that was a small price to pay. Clovis Andersen would undoubtedly have agreed with her, even if the author of *Theories of Crime,* who seemed to take a very high moral tone on all issues, might have had some misplaced reservations.

Mma Makutsi set to typing out the questionnaire. The questions were simple, but probing:

1. What are the main values which Africa can show to the world?

This question was designed to establish whether the girls knew what morality was all about. A morally aware girl would answer something along the lines: *Africa can show the world what it is to be human. Africa recognises the humanity of all people.*

Once they had negotiated this or, rather *if* they negotiated this, the next question would become more personal:

2. *What do you want to do with your life?*

This was where Mma Makutsi would trap any dishonest girl. The standard answer which any beauty contestant gave to this question was this: *I should like to work for charity, possibly with children. I would like to leave the world a better place than it was when I came into it.*

That was all very well, but they had all learned that answer from a book somewhere, possibly a book by somebody like Clovis Andersen. *Good Practice for Beauty Queens,* perhaps, or *How to Win in the World of Beauty Competitions.*

An honest girl, thought Mma Makutsi, would answer in something like the following fashion: *I wish to work for charity, possibly with children. If no children are available, I shall be happy to work with old people; I do not mind. But I am also keen to get a good job with a large salary.*

3. *Is it better to be beautiful than to be full of integrity?*

There was no doubt, again, that the answer which was expected of a beauty contestant was that integrity was more important. All the girls would probably feel that they had to say that, but there was a remote possibility that honesty would propel one into saying that being beautiful had its advantages. This was something that Mma Makutsi had noticed about secretarial jobs; beautiful girls were given all the jobs and there was very little left over for the rest, even if one had achieved 97 percent in the final examination. The injustice of this had always rankled, although in her own case, hard work had eventually paid off. How many of her contemporaries who may have had a better complexion than herself were now acting managers? The answer was undoubtedly none. Those beautiful girls married rich men, and lived in comfort thereafter, but they could hardly have claimed to have had careers—unless wearing expensive clothes and going to parties could be described as a career.

Mma Makutsi typed her questionnaire. There was no photocopier in the office, but she had used carbon paper and there were now four copies of the question sheet, with *Botswana Daily News Features Department* meretriciously typed at the top of the page. She looked at her watch; it was noon, and the day had warmed up uncomfortably. There had been some rain a few days previously, but this had rapidly been soaked up by the earth and the ground was crying out for more. If rain came, as it probably would, the temperatures would fall and people would feel comfortable again. Tempers became frayed in the hot season and arguments broke out about little things. Rain brought peace between people.

She went out of the office and closed the door behind her. The apprentices were busy with an old van which had been driven in by a woman who brought vegetables up from Lobatse to sell to the supermarkets. She had heard about the garage from a friend, who had said that it was a good place for a woman to take her vehicle.

"It is a ladies' garage, I think," the friend had said. "They understand ladies and they look after them well. It is the best place for a lady to take her car."

The acquisition of a reputation for looking after ladies' cars had kept the apprentices busy. Under Mma Makutsi's management, they had responded well to the challenge, working late hours and taking much greater care with their work. She checked up on them from time to time, and insisted that they explain to her exactly what they were doing. They enjoyed this, and it also helped to focus their thoughts on the problem before them. Their diagnostic power—so important a weapon in the armoury of any good mechanic—had improved greatly and they also wasted less time in idle chatter about girls.

"We like working for a woman," the older apprentice had said to her one morning. "It is a good thing to have a woman watching you all the time."

"I am very happy about that," said Mma Makutsi. "Your work is getting better and better all the time. One day you may be a famous mechanic like Mr J.L.B. Matekoni. That is always possible."

Now she walked over to the apprentices and watched them manipulating an oil filter.

"When you have finished that," she said, "I would like one of you to drive me over to the university."

"We are very busy, Mma," complained the younger one. "We have two more cars to see to today. We cannot go off here and there all the time. We are not taxi drivers."

Mma Makutsi sighed. "In that case I shall have to get a taxi. I have this important business to do with a beauty competition. I have to speak to some of the girls."

"I can drive you," said the older apprentice hurriedly. "I am almost ready. My brother here can finish this off."

"Good," said Mma Makutsi. "I knew that I could call on your finer nature."

THEY PARKED under a tree on the university campus, not far from the large, white-painted block to which Mma Makutsi had been directed when she showed the address to the man on the gate. A small group of female students stood chatting beneath a sun shelter that shaded the front door to the three-storey building. Leaving the apprentice in the van, Mma Makutsi made her way over to this group and introduced herself.

"I am looking for Motlamedi Matluli," she said. "I have been told she lives here."

One of the students giggled. "Yes, she lives here," she said. "Although I think that she would like to live somewhere a bit grander."

"Like the Sun Hotel," said another, causing them all to laugh.

MMA MAKUTSI smiled. "She is a very important girl, then?"

This brought forth more laughter. "She thinks she is," said one. "Just because she has all the boys running after her she thinks she owns Gaborone. You should just see her!"

"I would like to see her," said Mma Makutsi simply. "That is why I am here."

"You will find her in front of her mirror," said another. "She is on the first floor, in room 114."

Mma Makutsi thanked her informants and made her way up the concrete staircase to the first floor. She noticed that somebody had scribbled something uncomplimentary on the wall of the staircase, a remark about one of the girls. One of the male students, no doubt, had been rebuffed and had vented his feelings in graffiti. She felt annoyed; these people were privileged—ordinary people in Botswana would never have the chance to get this sort of education, which was all paid for by the Government, every pula and thebe of it—and all they could think of doing was writing on walls. And what was Motlamedi doing, spending time preening herself and entering beauty competitions when she should have been working on her books? If she were the Rector of the university she would tell people like that to make up their minds. You can be one thing or the other. You can cultivate your mind, or you can cultivate your hairstyle. But you cannot do both.

She found room 114 and knocked loudly on the door. There were sounds of a radio within and so she knocked again, louder this time.

"All right!" shouted a voice from within. "I'm coming."

The door was opened and Motlamedi Matluli stood before her. The first thing that struck Mma Makutsi about her was her eyes, which were extraordinarily large. They dominated the face, giving it a gentle, innocent quality, rather like the face of those small night creatures they called bush babies.

Motlamedi looked her visitor up and down.

"Yes Mma?" she asked casually. "What can I do for you?"

This was very rude, and Mma Makutsi smarted at the insult. If this girl had any manners, she would have invited me in, she thought. She is too busy with her mirror which, as the students below had predicted, was propped up on her desk and was surrounded by creams and lotions.

"I am a journalist," said Mma Makutsi. "I am writing an article about the finalists for Miss Beauty and Integrity. I have some questions I would like you to answer."

The change in Motlamedi's attitude was immediately apparent. Quickly, and rather effusively asking Mma Makutsi in, she cleared some clothes off a chair and invited her visitor to sit down.

"My room is not often this untidy," she laughed, gesturing to the piles of clothes that had been tossed down here and there.

"But I am just in the middle of sorting things out. You know how it is."

Mma Makutsi nodded. Taking the questionnaire out of her briefcase, she passed it over to the young woman who looked at it and smiled.

"These questions are very easy," she said. "I have seen questions like this before."

"Please fill them in," asked Mma Makutsi. "Then I would like to talk to you for a very short time before I leave you to get on with your studies."

The last remark was made as she looked about the room; it was, as far as she could make out, devoid of books.

"Yes," said Motlamedi, applying herself to the questionnaire, "we students are very busy with our studies."

While Motlamedi wrote out her answers, Mma Makutsi glanced discreetly at her head. Unfortunately the style in which the finalist had arranged her hair was such that it was impossible to see the shape of the head. Even Lombroso himself, thought Mma Makutsi, might have found it difficult to reach a view on this person. Yet this did not really matter; everything she had seen of this person, from her rudeness at the door to her look of near-disdain (concealed at the moment when Mma Makutsi had declared herself to be a journalist), told her that this woman would be a bad choice for the post of Miss Beauty and Integrity. She was unlikely to be charged with theft, of course, but there were other ways in which she could bring disgrace to the competition and to Mr Pulani. The most likely of these was involvement in some scandal with a married man; girls of this sort were no respecters of matrimony and could be expected to seek out any man who could advance her career, irrespective of whether he already had a wife. What sort of example would that be to the youth of Botswana? Mma Makutsi asked herself. The mere thought of it made her feel angry and she found herself involuntarily shaking her head with disapproval.

Motlamedi looked up from her form.

"What are you shaking your head about, Mma?" she asked. "Am I writing the wrong thing?"

"No, you are not." Her reply came hurriedly. "You must write the truth. That is all I am interested in."

Motlamedi smiled. "I always tell the truth," she said. "I have told the truth since I was a child. I cannot stand people who tell lies."

"Oh yes?"

She finished writing and handed the form to Mma Makutsi.

"I hope I have not written too much," she said. "I know that you journalists are very busy people."

Mma Makutsi took the form and ran her eye down the responses.

Question 1: Africa has a very great history, although many people pay no attention to it. Africa can teach the world about how to care for other people. There are other things, too, that Africa can teach the world.

Question 2: It is my greatest ambition to work for the benefit of other people. I look forward to the day when I can help more people. That is one of the reasons why I deserve to win this competition: I am a girl who likes to help people. I am not one of these selfish girls.

Question 3: It is better to be a person of integrity. An honest girl is rich in her heart. That is the truth. Girls who worry about their looks are not as happy as girls who think about other people first. I am one of these latter girls, and that is how I know this thing.

Motlamedi watched as Mma Makutsi read.

"Well, Mma?" she said. "Would you like to ask me about anything I have written?"

Mma Makutsi folded the sheet of paper and slipped it into her briefcase.

"No thank you, Mma," she said. "You have told me everything I need to know. I do not need to ask you any other questions."

Motlamedi looked anxious.

"What about a photograph?" she said. "If the paper would like to send a photographer I think that I could let a photograph be taken. I shall be here all afternoon."

Mma Makutsi moved towards the door.

"Perhaps," she said. "But I do not know. You have given me very useful answers here and I shall be able to put them into the newspaper. I feel I know you quite well now."

Motlamedi felt that she could now afford to be gracious.

"I am glad that we have met," she said. "I look forward to our next meeting. Maybe you will be at the competition . . . you could bring the photographer."

"Perhaps," said Mma Makutsi, as she left.

THE APPRENTICE was talking to a couple of young women when Mma Makutsi emerged. He was explaining something about the car and they were listening to him avidly. Mma Makutsi did not hear the entire conversation, but she did pick up the end: ". . . at least eighty miles an hour. And the engine is very quiet. If a boy is sitting with a girl in the back and wants to kiss her in that car he has to be very quiet because they will hear it in the front."

The students giggled.

"Do not listen to him, ladies," said Mma Makutsi. "This young man is not allowed to see girls. He already has a wife and three children and his wife gets very cross if she hears that girls are talking to him. Very cross."

The students moved back. One of them now looked at the apprentice reproachfully.

"But that is not true," protested the young man. "I am not married."

"That's what all you men say," said one of the students, angry now. "You come round here and talk to girls like us while all the time you are thinking of your wives. What sort of behaviour is that?"

"Very bad," chipped in Mma Makutsi, as she opened the passenger door and prepared to get in. "Anyway, it is time for us to go. This young man has to drive me somewhere else."

"You be careful of him, Mma," said one of the students. "We know about boys like that."

The apprentice started the car, tight-lipped, and drove off.

"You should not have said that, Mma. You made me look foolish."

Mma Makutsi snorted. "You made yourself look foolish. Why are you always running after girls? Why are you always trying to impress them?"

"Because that's how I enjoy myself," said the apprentice defensively. "I like talking to girls. We have all these beautiful girls in this country and there is nobody to talk to them. I am doing a service to the country."

Mma Makutsi looked at him scornfully. Although the young men had been working hard for her and had responded well to her suggestions, there seemed to be a chronic weakness in their character—this relentless womanising. Could anything be done about it? She doubted it, but it would pass in time, she thought, and they would become more serious. Or perhaps they would not. People did not change a great deal. Mma Ramotswe had said that to her once and it had stuck in her mind. People do not change, but that does not mean that they will always remain the same. What you can do is find out the good side of their character and then bring that out. Then it might seem that they had changed, which they had not; but they would be different afterwards, and better. That's what Mma Ramotswe had said—or something like that. And if there was one person in Botswana—one person—to whom one should listen very carefully, it was Mma Ramotswe.

CHAPTER SIXTEEN

THE COOK'S TALE

MMA RAMOTSWE lay on her bed and gazed up at the whiteboards of the ceiling. Her stomach felt less disturbed now, and the worst of the dizziness had passed. But when she shut her eyes, and then opened them again fairly shortly thereafter, there was a white ring about everything, a halo of light which danced for a moment and then dimmed. In other circumstances it might have been a pleasant sensation, but here, at the mercy of a poisoner, it was alarming. What substance would produce such a result? Poisons could attack eyesight, Mma Ramotswe knew that well. As a child they had been taught about the plants which could be harvested in the bush, the shrubs that could produce sleep, the tree bark which could bring an unwanted pregnancy to a sudden end, the roots that cured itching. But there were others, plants that produced the muti used by the witch doctors, innocent-looking plants which could kill at a touch, or so they were told. It was one of these, no doubt, that had been slipped onto her plate by her host's wife, or, more likely, put into an entire dish of food, indiscriminately, but avoided by the poisoner herself. If a person was wicked enough to poison a husband, then she would not stop at taking others with him.

Mma Ramotswe looked at her watch. It was past seven, and the windows were dark. She had slept through the sunset and now it was time for the evening meal, not that she felt like eating. They would be wondering where she was, though, and so she should tell them that she was unwell and could not join them for supper.

She sat up in her bed and blinked. The white light was still there, but was fading now. She put her feet over the edge of the bed and wriggled her toes into her shoes, hoping that no scorpions had crawled into them during her rest. She had always checked her shoes for scorpions since, as a child, she had put her foot into her school shoes one morning and had been badly stung by a large brown scorpion which had sheltered there for the night. Her entire foot had swollen up, so badly, in fact, that they had carried her to the Dutch Reformed Hospital at the foot of the hill. A nurse there had put on a dressing and given her something for the pain. Then she had warned her always to check her shoes and the warning had remained with her.

"We live up here," said the nurse, holding her hand at chest height. "They live down there. Remember that."

Later, it had seemed to her that this was a warning that could apply in more senses than one. Not only did it refer to scorpions and snakes—about which it was patently true—but it could apply with equal force to people. There was a world beneath the world inhabited by ordinary, law-abiding people; a world of selfishness and mistrust occupied by scheming and manipulative people. One had to check one's shoes.

She withdrew her toes from the shoes before they had reached the end. Reaching down, she picked up the right shoe and tipped it up. There was nothing. She picked up the left shoe and did the same. Out dropped a tiny glistening creature, which danced on the floor for a moment, as if in defiance, and then scuttled off into the dark of a corner.

Mma Ramotswe made her way down the corridor. As she reached the end, where the corridor became a living room, the maid came out of a doorway and greeted her.

"I was coming to find you, Mma," said the maid. "They have made food and it is almost ready."

"Thank you, Mma. I have been sleeping. I have not been feeling well, although I am better now. I do not think that I could eat tonight, but I would like some tea. I'm very thirsty."

The maid's hands shot up to her mouth. "Aiee! That is very bad, Mma! All of the people have been ill. The old lady has been sick, sick, all the time. The man and his wife have been shouting out and holding their stomachs. Even the boy was sick, although he was not so bad. The meat must have been bad."

MMA RAMOTSWE stared at the maid. "Everybody?"

"Yes. Everybody. The man was shouting that he would go and chase the butcher who sold that meat. He was very cross."

"And the wife? What was she doing?"

The maid looked down at the floor. These were intimate matters of the human stomach and it embarrassed her to talk about them so openly.

"She could keep nothing down. She tried to take water—I brought it to her—but it came straight up again. Her stomach is now empty, though, and I think she is feeling better. I have been a nurse all afternoon. Here, there. I even looked in through your door to see that you were all right and I saw you sleeping peacefully. I did not know that you had been sick too."

Mma Ramotswe was silent for a moment. The information which the maid had given her changed the situation entirely. The principal suspect, the wife, had been poisoned, as had the old woman, who was also a suspect. This meant either that there had been an accident in the distribution of the poison, or that neither of these had anything to do with it. Of the two possibilities, Mma Ramotswe thought that the second was the more likely. When she had been feeling ill she imagined that she had been deliberately poisoned, but was this likely? On sober reflection, beyond the waves of nausea that had engulfed her, it seemed ridiculous to think that a poisoner would strike so quickly, and so obviously, on the arrival of a guest. It would have been suspicious and unsubtle, and poisoners, she had read, were usually extremely subtle people.

The maid looked at Mma Ramotswe expectantly, as if she thought that the guest might now take over the running of the household.

"None of them needs a doctor, do they?" asked Mma Ramotswe.

"No. They are all getting better, I think. But I do not know what to do. They shout at me a lot and I cannot do anything when they are all shouting."

"No," said Mma Ramotswe. "That would not be easy for you."

She looked at the maid. They shout at me a lot. Here was

another with a motive, she reflected, but the thought was absurd. This was an honest woman. Her face was open and she smiled as she spoke. Secrets left shadows on the face, and there were none there.

"Well," said Mma Ramotswe, "you could make me some tea, perhaps. Then, after that, I think you should go off to your room and leave them to get better. Perhaps they will shout less in the morning."

The maid smiled appreciatively. "I will do that, Mma. I will bring you your tea in your room. Then you can go back to sleep."

SHE SLEPT, but fitfully. From time to time she awoke, and heard voices from within the house, or the sounds of movement, a door slamming, a window being opened, the creaking noises of an old house by night. Shortly before dawn, when she realised that she would not fall asleep, she arose, slipped on her house-coat, and made her way out of the house. A dog at the back door rose to its feet, still groggy with sleep, and sniffed suspiciously at her feet; a large bird, which had been perched on the roof, launched itself with an effort and flew away.

Mma Ramotswe looked about her. The sun would not be up for half an hour or so, but there was enough light to make things out and it grew stronger and clearer every moment. The trees were still indistinct, dark shapes, but the branches and the leaves would soon appear in detail, like a painting revealed. It was a time of day that she loved, and here, in this lonely spot, away from roads and people and the noise they made, the loveliness of her land appeared distilled. The sun would come before too long and coarsen the world; for the moment, though, the bush, the sky, the earth itself, seemed modest and understated.

Mma Ramotswe took a deep breath. The smell of the bush, the smell of the dust and the grass, caught at her heart, as it always did; and now there was added a whiff of wood smoke, that marvellous, acrid smell that insinuates itself through the still air of morning as people make their breakfast and warm their hands at the flames. She turned around. There was a fire nearby; the morning fire to heat the hot water boiler, or the fire, perhaps, of a watchman who had spent the night hours around a few burning embers.

She walked round to the back of the house, following a small path which had been marked out with whitewashed stones, a habit picked up from the colonial administrators who had whitewashed the stones surrounding their encampments and quarters. They had done this throughout Africa, even whitewashing the lower trunks of the trees they had planted in long avenues. Why? Because of Africa.

She turned the corner of the house and saw the man crouched before the old brick-encased boiler. Such boilers were common features of older houses, which had no electricity, and of course they were still necessary out here, where there was no power apart from that provided by the generator. It would be far cheaper to heat the household's water in such a boiler than to use the diesel-generated current. And here was the boiler being stoked up with wood to make hot water for the morning baths.

The man saw her approaching and stood up, wiping his khaki trousers as he did so. Mma Ramotswe greeted him in the traditional way and he replied courteously. He was a tall man in his early forties, well-built, and he had strong, good-looking features.

"You are making a good fire there, Rra," she observed, pointing to the glow that came from the front of the boiler.

"The trees here are good for burning," he said simply. "There are many of them. We never lack for firewood."

Mma Ramotswe nodded. "So this is your job?"

He frowned. "That and other things."

"Oh?" The tone of his remark intrigued her. These "other things" were clearly unwelcome. "What other things, Rra?"

"I am the cook," he said. "I am in charge of the kitchen and I make the food."

He looked at her defensively, as if expecting a response.

"That is good," said Mma Ramotswe. "It is a good thing to be able to cook. They have got some very fine men cooks down in Gaborone. They call them chefs and they wear peculiar white hats."

The man nodded. "I used to work in a hotel in Gaborone," he said. "I was a cook there. Not the head cook, but one of the junior ones. That was a few years ago."

"Why did you come here?" asked Mma Ramotswe. It seemed an extraordinary thing to have done. Cooks like that in Gaborone would have been paid far more, she assumed, than cooks in the farmhouses.

The cook stretched out a leg and pushed a piece of wood back into the fire with his foot.

"I never liked it," he said. "I did not like being a cook then, and I do not like it now."

"Then why do it, Rra?"

He sighed. "It is a difficult story, Mma. To tell it would take a long time, and I have to get back to work when the sun comes up. But I can tell you some of it now, if you like. You sit down there, Mma, on that log. Yes. That is fine. I shall tell you since you ask me.

"I come from over that way, by that hill, over there, but behind it, ten miles behind it. There is a village there which nobody knows because it is not important and nothing ever happens there. Nobody pays attention to it because the people there are very quiet. They never shout and they never make a fuss. So nothing ever happens.

"There was a school in the village with a very wise teacher. He had two other teachers to help him, but he was the main one, and everybody listened to him rather than the other teachers. He said to me one day, 'Samuel, you are a very clever boy. You can remember the names of all the cattle and who the mothers and fathers of the cattle were. You are better than anybody else at that. A boy like you could go to Gaborone and get a job.'

"I did not find it strange that I should remember cattle as I loved cattle more than anything else. I wanted to work with cattle one day, but there was no work with cattle where we were and so I had to think of something else. I did not believe that I was good enough to go to Gaborone, but when I was sixteen the teacher gave me some money which the Government had given him and I used it to buy a bus ticket to Gaborone. My father had no money, but he gave me a watch which he had found one day lying beside the edge of the tarred road. It was his prize possession, but he gave it to me and told me to sell it for money to buy food once I reached Gaborone.

"I did not want to sell that watch, but eventually, when my

stomach was so empty that it was sore, I had to do so. I was given one hundred pula for it, because it was a good watch, and I spent that on food to make me strong.

"It took me many days to find work, and my money for food would not last forever. At last I found work in a hotel, where they made me carry things and open doors for guests. Sometimes these guests came from very far away, and they were very rich. Their pockets were full of money. They gave me tips sometimes, and I saved the money in the post office. I wish I still had that money.

"After a while, they transferred me to the kitchen, where I helped the chefs. They found out that I was a good cook and they gave me a uniform. I cooked there for ten years, although I hated it. I did not like those hot kitchens and all those smells of food, but it was my job, and I had to do it. And it was while I was doing that, working in that hotel, that I met the brother of the man who lives here. You may know the one I am talking about—he is the important one who lives in Gaborone. He said that he would give me a job up here, as Assistant Manager of the farm, and I was very happy. I told him that I knew all about cattle, and that I would look after the farm well.

"I came up here with my wife. She is from this part, and she was very happy to be back. They gave us a nice place to live, and my wife is now very contented. You will know, Mma, how important it is to have a wife or a husband who is contented. If you do not, then you will never have any peace. Never. I also have a contented mother-in-law. She moved in and lives at the back of the house. She is always singing because she is so happy that she has her daughter and my children there.

"I was looking forward to working with the cattle, but as

soon as I met the brother who lives up here, he asked me what I had done and I said that I had been a cook. He was very pleased to hear this and he said that I should be the cook in the house. They were always having big, important people up from Gaborone and it would impress them if there was a real cook in the house. I said that I did not want to do this, but he forced me. He spoke to my wife and she took his side. She said that this was such a good place to be that only a fool would not do what these people wanted me to do. My mother-in-law started to wail. She said that she was an old woman and she would die if we had to move. My wife said to me: 'Do you want to kill my mother? Is that what you are wanting to do?'

"So I have had to be the cook in this place, and I am still surrounded by cooking smells when I would rather be out with the cattle. That is why I am not contented, Mma, when all my family is very contented. It is a strange story, do you not think?"

HE FINISHED the story and looked mournfully at Mma Ramotswe. She met his gaze, and then looked away. She was thinking, her mind racing ahead of itself, the possibilities jostling one another until a hypothesis emerged, was examined, and a conclusion reached.

She looked at him again. He had risen to his feet and was closing the door of the boiler. Within the water tank, an old petrol drum converted for the purpose, she heard the bubbling of heating water. Should she speak, or should she remain silent? If she spoke, she could be wrong and he could take violent exception to what she said. But if she held back, then she would have lost the moment. So she decided.

"There's something that I've been wanting to ask you, Rra," she said.

"Yes?" He glanced up at her briefly, and then busied himself again with the tidying of the wood stack.

"I saw you putting something into the food yesterday. You didn't see me, but I saw you. Why did you do it?"

He froze. He was on the point of lifting up a large log, his hands stretched around it, his back bent, ready to take the weight. Then, quite slowly, his hands unclasped and he straightened himself up.

"You saw me?" His voice was strained, almost inaudible.

Mma Ramotswe swallowed. "Yes. I saw you. You put something in the food. Something bad."

He looked at her now, and she saw that the eyes had dulled. The face, animated before, was devoid of expression.

"You are not trying to kill them, are you?"

He opened his mouth to answer, but no sound came.

Mma Ramotswe felt emboldened. She had made the right decision and now she had to finish what she had begun.

"You just wanted them to stop using you as a cook, didn't you? If they felt that your food tasted bad, then they would just give up on you as a cook and you could get back to the work that you really wanted to do. That's right, isn't it?"

He nodded.

"You were very foolish, Rra," said Mma Ramotswe. "You could have harmed somebody."

"Not with what I used," he said. "It was perfectly safe."

Mma Ramotswe shook her head. "It is never safe."

The cook looked down at his hands.

"I am not a murderer," he said. "I am not that sort of man."

Mma Ramotswe snorted. "You are very lucky that I worked out what you were doing," she said. "I didn't see you, of course, but your story gave you away."

"And now?" said the cook. "You will tell them and they will call the police. Please, Mma, remember that I have a family. If I cannot work for these people it will be hard for me to find another job now. I am getting older. I cannot . . ."

Mma Ramotswe raised a hand to stop him. "I am not that sort of person," she said. "I am going to tell them that the food you used was bad, but that you could not tell it. I am going to tell the brother that he should give you another job."

"He will not do that," said the cook. "I have asked him."

"But I am a woman," said Mma Ramotswe. "I know how to make men do things."

The cook smiled. "You are very kind, Mma."

"Too kind," said Mma Ramotswe, turning to go back towards the house. The sun was beginning to come up and the trees and the hills and the very earth were golden. It was a beautiful place to be, and she would have liked to have stayed. But now there was nothing more to do. She knew what she had to tell the Government Man and she might as well return to Gaborone to do it.

CHAPTER SEVENTEEN

AN EXCELLENT TYPE OF GIRL

IT HAD not been difficult to identify Motlamedi as unsuitable for the important office of Miss Beauty and Integrity. There were three further names on the list, though, and each of them would have to be interviewed for a judgement to be made. They might not be so transparent; it was rare for Mma Makutsi to feel sure about somebody on a first meeting, but there was no doubt in her mind that Motlamedi was, quite simply, a *bad girl*. This description was very specific; it had nothing to do with *bad women* or *bad ladies*—they were quite different categories. Bad women were prostitutes; bad ladies were manipulative older ladies, usually married to older men, who interfered in the affairs of others for their own selfish ends. The expression *bad girl,* by contrast, referred to somebody who was usually rather younger (certainly under thirty) and whose interest was in having a good time. That was the essence of it, in fact—a good time. Indeed there was a subcategory of bad girls, that of *good-time girls.* These were girls who were mainly to be found in bars with flashy men, having what appeared to be a good time. Some of these flashy men, of course, saw themselves as merely being *one of the boys,* which they thought gave them an excuse for all sorts of selfish behaviour. But not in Mma Makutsi's book.

At the other end of the spectrum, there were *good girls.* These were girls who worked hard and who were appreciated by their families. They were the ones who visited the elders; who looked after the smaller children, sitting for hours under a tree watching the children play; and who in due course trained to be nurses or, as in Mma Makutsi's case, undertook a general secretarial training at the Botswana Secretarial College. Unfortunately, these good girls, who carried half the world upon their shoulders, did not have much fun.

There was no doubt that Motlamedi was not a good girl, but was there any possibility, Mma Makutsi now glumly asked herself, that any of the others might prove to be much better? The difficulty was that good girls were unlikely to enter a beauty competition in the first place. It was, in general, not the sort of thing that good girls thought of doing. And if her pessimism were to prove justified, then what would she be able to say to Mr Pulani when he came to her for her report? It would not be very useful to say that all the girls were as bad as one another, that none of them was worthy of the title. That would be singularly unhelpful, and she suspected that she would not even be able to put in a fee note for that sort of information.

She sat in her car with the apprentice and looked despairingly at her list of names.

"Where to now?" asked the apprentice. His tone was surly,

but only just so; he realised that she was, after all, still Acting Manager, and both he and his colleague had a healthy respect for this remarkable woman who had come to the garage and turned their working practices upside down.

Mma Makutsi sighed. "I have three girls to see," she said. "And I cannot decide which one to go to next."

The apprentice laughed. "I know a lot about girls," he said. "I could tell you."

Mma Makutsi cast a scornful glance in his direction. "You and your girls!" she said. "That's all you think of, isn't it? You and that lazy friend of yours. Girls, girls, girls . . ."

She stopped herself. Yes, he was an expert in girls—it was well-known—and Gaborone was not such a large place. There was a chance, probably quite a good chance, that he actually knew something about these girls. If they were bad girls, as they almost certainly were, or, more specifically, good-time girls, then he would probably have encountered them on his rounds of the bars. She signalled for him to draw over to the side of the road.

"Stop. Stop here. I want to show you this list."

The apprentice drew in and took the list from Mma Makutsi. As he read it, he broke into a smile.

"This is a fine list of girls!" he said enthusiastically. "These are some of the best girls in town. Or at least three of them are the best girls in town. Big girls, you know what I mean, big, excellent girls. These are girls that we boys are very appreciative of. We approve of these girls. Oh yes! Too much!"

Mma Makutsi's heart skipped a beat. Her intuition had been right; he had the answer to her quest and now all that she had to do was to coax it out of him.

"So which girls do you know?" she asked. "Which are the three you know?"

The apprentice laughed. "This one here," he said. "This one who is called Makita. I know her. She is very good fun, and she laughs a lot, especially when you tickle her. Then this one, Gladys, my, my! Ow! One, two, three! And I also know this one here, this girl called Motlamedi, or rather my brother knows her. He says that she is a very clever girl who is a student at the university but she doesn't waste too much time on her books. Lots of brains, but also a very big bottom. She is more interested in being glamorous."

Mma Makutsi nodded. "I have just been speaking to that girl," she said. "Your brother is right about her. But what about that other girl, Patricia, the one who lives in Tlokweng? Do you know that girl?"

The apprentice shook his head. "She is an unknown girl that one," he said, adding quickly, "But I am sure that she is a very charming girl, too. You never know."

Mma Makutsi took the piece of paper away from him and tucked it into the pocket of her dress. "We are going to Tlokweng," she said. "I need to meet this Patricia."

They drove out to Tlokweng in silence. The apprentice appeared to be lost in thought—possibly thinking about the girls on the list—while Mma Makutsi was thinking about the apprentice. It was very unfair—but entirely typical of the injustice of the relations between the sexes—that there was no expression quite like *good-time girl* that could be applied to boys like this ridiculous apprentice. They were every bit as bad—if not worse—as the *good-time girls* themselves, but nobody seemed to blame them for it. Nobody spoke of *bar boys*, for example, and nobody would describe any male over twelve as a *bad boy*. Women, as usual, were expected to behave better than men, and inevitably attracted criticism for doing things that men were licensed to do with impunity. It was not fair; it had never been fair, and it would probably never be fair in the future. Men would wriggle out of it somehow, even if you tied them up in a constitution. Men judges would find that the constitution really said something rather different from what was written on the page and interpret it in a favour of men. *All people, both men and women, are entitled to equal treatment in the workplace* became *Women can get some jobs, but they cannot do certain jobs (for their own protection) as men will do these jobs better anyway.*

Why did men behave like this? It had always been a mystery to Mma Makutsi although latterly she had begun to glimpse the makings of an explanation. She thought that it might have something to do with the way in which mothers treated their sons. If the mothers allowed the boys to think that they were special—and all mothers did that, as far as Mma Makutsi could make out—then that encouraged boys to develop attitudes which never left them. If young boys were allowed to think that women were there to look after them, then they would continue to think this when they grew up—and they did. Mma Makutsi had seen so many examples of it that she could not imagine anybody seriously challenging the theory. This very apprentice was an example. She had seen his mother come to the garage once with a whole watermelon for her son and she had seen her cut it for him and give it to him in the way in which one would feed a small child. That mother should not be doing that; she should be encouraging her son to buy his own watermelons and cut them up himself. It was exactly this sort of treatment which made him so immature in his treatment of women. They were playthings to him; hewers of watermelon; eternal substitute mothers.

THEY ARRIVED at plot 2456, at the gate of the neat, mud-brown little house with its outhouse for the chickens and, unusually, two traditional grain bins at the back. The chicken food would be kept there, she thought; the sorghum grain that would be scattered each morning on the neatly swept yard, to be pecked at by the hungry birds on their release from the coop. It was obvious to Mma Makutsi that an older woman lived here, as only an older woman would take the trouble to keep the yard in such a traditional and careful way. She would be Patricia's grandmother, perhaps—one of those remarkable African women who worked and worked into her eighties, and beyond, and who were the very heart of the family.

The apprentice parked the car while Mma Makutsi made her way up the path that led to the house. She had called out, as was polite, but she thought that they had not heard her; now a woman appeared at the door, wiping her hands on a cloth and greeting her warmly.

Mma Makutsi explained her mission. She did not say that she was a journalist, as she had done on the visit to Motlamedi; it would have been wrong to do that here, in this traditional home, to the woman who had revealed herself to be Patricia's mother.

"I want to find out about the people in this competition," she said. "I have been asked to talk to them."

The woman nodded. "We can sit at the doorway," she said. "It is shady. I will call my daughter. That is her room there."

She pointed to a door at the side of the house. The green paint which had once covered it was peeling off and the hinges looked rusty. Although the yard appeared well kept, the house itself seemed to be in need of repair. There was not a great deal of money about, thought Mma Makutsi, and pondered, for a moment, what the cash prize for the eventually elected Miss Beauty and Integrity could mean in circumstances such as these. That prize was four thousand pula, and a voucher to spend in a clothing store. Not much of the money would be wasted, thought Mma Makutsi, noticing the frayed hem of the woman's skirt.

She sat down and took the mug of water which the woman had offered her.

"It is hot today," said the woman. "But there will be rain soon. I am sure of that."

"There will be rain," agreed Mma Makutsi. "We need the rain."

"We do need it, Mma," said the woman. "This country always needs rain."

"You are right, Mma. Rain."

They were silent for a moment, thinking about rain. When there was no rain, you thought about it, hardly daring to hope for the miracle to begin. And when the rain came, all you could think about was how long it would last. *God is crying. God is crying for this country. See, children, there are his tears. The rain is his tears.* That is what the teacher at Bobonong had said one day, when she was young, and she had remembered her words.

"Here is my daughter."

Mma Makutsi looked up. Patricia had appeared silently and was standing before her. She smiled at the younger woman, who dropped her eyes and gave a slight curtsey. *I am not that old!* thought Mma Makutsi, but she was impressed by the gesture.

"You can sit down," said her mother. "This lady wants to talk to you about the beauty competition."

Patricia nodded. "I am very excited about it, Mma. I know that I won't win, but I am still very excited."

Don't be too sure about that, thought Mma Makutsi, but did not say anything.

"Her aunt has made her a very nice dress for the competition," said the mother. "She has spent a lot of money on it and it is very fine material. It is a very good dress."

"But the other girls will be more beautiful," said Patricia. "They are very smart girls. They live in Gaborone. There is even one who is a student at the university. She is a very clever girl that one."

And bad, thought Mma Makutsi.

"You must not think that you will lose," interjected the mother. "That is not the way to go into a competition. If you think that you will lose, then you will never win. What if Seretse Khama had said: We will never get anywhere. Then where would Botswana be today? Where would it be?"

Mma Makutsi nodded her agreement. "That is no way to set out," she said. "You must think: I can win. Then you may win. You never know."

Patricia smiled. "You are right. I shall try to be more determined. I shall do my best."

"Good," said Mma Makutsi. "Now tell me, what would you like to do with your life?"

There was a silence. Both Mma Makutsi and the mother looked expectantly at Patricia.

"I would like to go to the Botswana Secretarial College," replied Patricia.

Mma Makutsi looked at her, watching her eyes. She was not lying. This was a wonderful girl, a truthful girl, one of the finest girls in Botswana, quite beyond any doubt.

"That is a very fine college," she said. "I am a graduate of it myself." She paused, and then decided to go ahead. "In fact, I got 97 percent there."

Patricia sucked in her breath. "Ow! That is a very high mark, Mma. You must be very clever."

Mma Makutsi laughed dismissively. "Oh no, I worked hard. That was all."

"But it is very good," said Patricia. "You are very lucky, Mma, to be pretty and clever too."

Mma Makutsi was at a loss for words. She had not been called pretty before, or not by a stranger. Her aunts had said that she should try to make something of what looks she had, and her mother had made a similar remark; but nobody had called her pretty, except this young woman, still in her late teens, who was herself so obviously pretty.

"You are very kind," she said.

"She is a kind girl," said the mother. "She has always been a kind girl."

Mma Makutsi smiled. "Good," she said. "And do you know something? I think that she has a very good chance of winning that competition. In fact, I am sure that she is going to win. I am sure of it."

CHAPTER EIGHTEEN

THE FIRST STEP

MMA RAMOTSWE returned to Gaborone on the morning of her conversation with the cook. There had been further conversations—prolonged in one case—with other members of the household. She had talked to the new wife, who had listened gravely, and had hung her head. She had spoken to the old woman, who had been proud at first, and unbending, but who had eventually acknowledged the truth of what Mma Ramotswe had told her and had agreed with her in the end. And then she had confronted the brother, who had stared at her open-mouthed, but who had taken his cue from his mother, who had intruded into the conversation and told him sharply where his duty lay. At the end of it Mma Ramotswe felt raw; she had taken such risks, but her intuition had proved her correct and her strategy had paid off. There was only one more person to speak to now, and that person was back in Gaborone and he, she feared, might not be so easy.

The drive back was a pleasant one. The previous day's rains had already had an effect and there was a tinge of green across the land. In one or two places, there were puddles of water in which the sky was reflected in patches of silver blue. And the dust had been laid, which was perhaps most refreshing of all; that omnipresent, fine dust that towards the end of the dry season would get everywhere, clogging everything up and making one's clothes stiff and uncomfortable.

She drove straight back to Zebra Drive, where the children greeted her excitedly, the boy rushing round the tiny white van with whoops of delight and the girl propelling her wheelchair out onto the drive to meet her. And in the kitchen window, staring out at her, the face of Rose, her maid, who had looked after the children over her brief absence.

Rose made tea while Mma Ramotswe heard the children tell her of what had happened at school. There had been a competition and a classmate had won a prize of a fifty pula book token. One of the teachers had broken his arm and had appeared with the injured limb in a sling. A girl in one of the junior classes had eaten a whole tube of toothpaste and had been sick, which was only to be expected, was it not?

But there was other news. Mma Makutsi had telephoned from the office and had asked Mma Ramotswe to call back the moment she arrived home, which she had thought would be the following day.

"She sounded very excited," said Rose. "She said there was something important she wanted to talk to you about."

A steaming cup of bush tea before her, Mma Ramotswe dialled the number of Tlokweng Road Speedy Motors, the number shared by the two offices. The telephone rang for some time before she heard the familiar voice of Mma Makutsi.

"The No. 1 Tlokweng Road . . ." she began. "No. The No. 1 Speedy Ladies' . . ."

"It's just me, Mma," said Mma Ramotswe. "And I know what you mean."

"I am always getting the two mixed up," said Mma Makutsi, laughing. "That's what comes of trying to run two businesses at the same time."

"I am sure that you have been running both very well," said Mma Ramotswe.

"Well, yes," said Mma Makutsi. "In fact, I telephoned you to tell you that I have just collected a very large fee. Two thousand pula for one case. The client was very happy."

"You have done very well," said Mma Ramotswe. "I shall come in later and see just how well you have done. But first I would like you to arrange an appointment for me. Telephone that Government Man and tell him that he must come and see me at four o'clock."

"And if he's busy?"

"Tell him that he cannot be busy. Tell him that this matter is too important to wait."

She finished her tea and then ate a large meat sandwich which Rose had prepared for her. Mma Ramotswe had got out of the habit of a cooked lunch, except at weekends, and was happy with a snack or a glass of milk. She had a taste for sugar, however, and this meant that a doughnut or a cake might follow the sandwich. She was a traditionally built lady, after all, and she did not have to worry about dress size, unlike those poor, neurotic people who were always looking in mirrors and thinking that they were too big. What was too big, anyway? Who was to tell another person what size they should be? It was a form of dictatorship, by the thin, and she was not having any of it. If these thin people became any more insistent, then the more generously sized people would just have to sit on them. Yes, that would teach them! Hah!

It was shortly before three when she arrived at the office. The apprentices were busy with a car, but greeted her warmly and with none of the sullen resentment which had so annoyed her in the past.

"You're very busy," she said. "That is a very nice car that you're fixing there."

The older apprentice wiped his mouth with his sleeve. "It is a wonderful car. It belongs to a lady. Do you know that all the ladies are bringing their cars here now? We are so busy that we will need to take on apprentices ourselves! That will be a fine thing! We shall have desks and an office and there will be apprentices running round doing what we tell them to do."

"You are a very amusing young man," said Mma Ramotswe, smiling. "But do not get too big for your boots. Remember that you are just an apprentice and that the lady in there with the glasses is the boss now."

The apprentice laughed. "She is a good boss. We like her." He paused for a moment, looking intently at Mma Ramotswe. "But what about Mr J.L.B. Matekoni? Is he getting better?"

"It is too early to say," Mma Ramotswe replied. "Dr Moffat said that these pills could take two weeks. We have a few days to wait before we can tell."

"He is being well looked after?"

Mma Ramotswe nodded. The fact that the apprentice had asked that question was a good sign. It suggested that he was beginning to take an interest in the welfare of others. Perhaps he was growing up. Perhaps it was something to do with Mma Makutsi, who might have been teaching them a bit about morality as well as a bit about hard work.

She entered the office, to find Mma Makutsi on the telephone. She finished the conversation quickly and rose to greet her employer.

"Here it is," said Mma Makutsi, handing a piece of paper to Mma Ramotswe.

Mma Ramotswe looked at the cheque. Two thousand pula, it seemed, awaited the No. 1 Ladies' Detective Agency at the Standard Bank. And at the bottom of the cheque was the well-known name that made Mma Ramotswe draw in her breath.

"The beauty contest man . . . ?"

"That's him," said Mma Makutsi. "He was the client."

Mma Ramotswe tucked the cheque safely away in her bodice. Modern business methods were all very well, she thought, but when it came to the safeguarding of money there were some places which had yet to be bettered.

"You must have worked very quickly," said Mma Ramotswe. "What was the problem? Wife difficulties?"

"No," said Mma Makutsi. "It was all about beautiful girls and the finding of a beautiful girl who could be trusted."

"Very intriguing," said Mma Ramotswe. "And you obviously found one."

"Yes," said Mma Makutsi. "I found the right one to win his competition."

Mma Ramotswe was puzzled, but there was not enough time to go into it as she had to prepare herself for her four o'clock appointment. Over the next hour, she dealt with the mail, helped Mma Makutsi file papers relating to the garage, and drank a quick cup of bush tea. By the time that the large black car drew up outside the office and disgorged the Government Man, the office was tidy and organised and Mma Makutsi, seated primly behind her desk, was pretending to type a letter.

"SO!" SAID the Government Man, leaning back in the chair and folding his hands across his stomach. "You didn't stay very long up there. I take it that you managed to catch that poisoner. I very much hope that you did!"

Mma Ramotswe glanced at Mma Makutsi. They were used to male arrogance, but this far surpassed the normal such display.

"I spent exactly as much time up there as I needed to, Rra," she said calmly. "Then I came back to discuss the case with you."

The Government Man's lip curled. "I want an answer, Mma. I have not come to conduct a long conversation."

The typewriter clicked sharply in the background. "In that case," said Mma Ramotswe, "you can go back to your office. You either want to hear what I have to say, or you don't."

The Government Man was silent. Then he spoke, his voice lowered. "You are a very insolent woman. Perhaps you do not have a husband who can teach you how to speak to men with respect."

The noise from the typewriter rose markedly.

"And perhaps you need a wife who can teach you how to speak to women with respect," said Mma Ramotswe. "But do not let me hold you up. The door is there, Rra. It is open. You can go now."

The Government Man did not move.

"Did you hear what I said, Rra? Am I going to have to throw you out? I have got two young men out there who are very strong from all that work with engines. Then there is Mma Makutsi, whom you didn't even greet by the way, and there is me. That makes four people. Your driver is an old man. You are outnumbered, Rra."

Still the Government Man did not move. His eyes now were fixed on the floor.

"Well, Rra?" Mma Ramotswe drummed her fingers on the table.

The Government Man looked up.

"I am sorry, Mma. I have been rude."

"Thank you," said Mma Ramotswe. "Now, after you have greeted Mma Makutsi properly, in the traditional way, please, then we shall begin."

"I AM going to tell you a story," said Mma Ramotswe to the Government Man. "This story begins when there was a family with three sons. The father was very pleased that his firstborn was a son and he gave him everything that he wanted. The mother of this boy was also pleased that she had borne a boy for her husband, and she also made a fuss of this boy. Then another boy was born, and it was very sad for them when they realised that this boy had something wrong with his head. The mother heard what people were saying behind her back, that the reason why the boy was like that was that she had been with another man while she was pregnant. This was not true, of course, but all those wicked words cut and cut at her and she was ashamed to be seen out. But that boy was happy; he liked to be with cattle and to count them, although he could not count very well.

"The firstborn was very clever and did well. He went to Gaborone and he became well-known in politics. But as he became more powerful and well-known, he became more and more arrogant.

"But another son had been born. The firstborn was very happy with this, and he loved that younger boy. But underneath the love, there was fear that this new boy would take away the love that he himself had in the family and that the father would prefer him. Everything that the father did was seen as a sign that he preferred this youngest son, which was not true, of course, because the old man loved all his sons.

"When the youngest son took a wife, the firstborn was very angry. He did not tell anybody that he was angry, but that anger was bubbling away inside him. He was too proud to talk to anybody about it, because he had become so important and so big. He thought that this new wife would take his brother away from him, and then he would be left with nothing. He thought that she would try to take away their farm and all their cattle. He did not bother to ask himself whether this was true.

"He began to believe that she was planning to kill his brother, the brother whom he loved so much. He could not sleep for thinking of this, because there was so much hate growing up within him. So at last he went to see a certain lady—and I am that lady—and asked her to go and find proof that this was what was happening. He thought in this way that she might help him to get rid of the brother's wife.

"The lady did not know then what lay behind all this, and so she went up to stay with this unhappy family on their farm.

She spoke to them all and she found out that nobody was trying to kill anybody and that all this talk about poison had come up only because there was an unhappy cook who got his herbs mixed up. This man had been made unhappy by the brother because he had been forced to do things that he did not want to do. So the lady from Gaborone spoke to all the members of the family, one by one. Then she came back to Gaborone and spoke to the brother. He was very rude to her, because he had developed habits of rudeness and because he always got his own way. But she realised that under the skin of a bully there is always a person who is frightened and unhappy. And this lady thought that she would speak to that frightened and unhappy person.

"She knew, of course, that he would be unable to speak to his own family himself, and so she had done so for him. She told the family how he felt, and how his love for his brother had made him act jealously. The wife of his brother understood and she promised that she would do everything in her power to make him feel that she had not taken his beloved brother away from him. Then the mother understood too; she realised that she and her husband had made him feel anxious about losing his share of the farm and that they would attend to that. They said that they would make sure that everything was divided equally and that he need have no fear for what would happen in the future.

"Then this lady said to the family that she would talk to the brother in Gaborone and that she was sure that he would understand. She said that she would pass on to him any words that they might wish to say. She said that the real poison within families is not the poison that you put in your food, but the poison that grows up in the heart when people are jealous of one another and cannot speak these feelings and drain out the poison that way.

"So she came back to Gaborone with some words that the family wanted to say. And the words of the youngest brother were these: *I love my brother very much. I will never forget him. I would never take anything from him. The land and the cattle are for sharing with him.* And the wife of this man said: *I admire the brother of my husband and I would never take away from him the brother's love that he deserves to have.* And the mother said: *I am very proud of my son. There is room here for all of us. I have been worried that my sons will grow apart and that their wives will come between them and break up our family. I am not worried about that anymore. Please ask my son to come and see me soon. I do not have much time.* And the old father did not say very much except: *No man could ask for better sons.*"

THE TYPEWRITER was silent. Now Mma Ramotswe stopped speaking and watched the Government Man, who sat quite still, only his chest moving slightly as he breathed in and out. Then he raised a hand slowly to his face, and leant forward. He raised his other hand to his face.

"Do not be ashamed to cry, Rra," said Mma Ramotswe. "It is the way that things begin to get better. It is the first step."

CHAPTER NINETEEN

THE WORDS FOR AFRICA

THERE WAS rain over the next four days. Every afternoon the clouds built up and then, amid bolts of lightning and great clashes of thunder, the rain fell upon the land. The roads, normally so dry and dusty, were flooded and the fields were shimmering expanses. But the thirsty land soon soaked up the water and the ground reappeared; but at least the people knew that the water was there, safely stored in the dam, and percolating down into the soil into which their wells were sunk. Everybody seemed relieved; another drought would have been too much to bear, although people would have put up with it, as they always had. The weather, they said, was changing and everybody felt vulnerable. In a country like Botswana, where the land and the animals were on such a narrow margin, a slight change could be disastrous. But the rains had come, and that was the important thing.

Tlokweng Road Speedy Motors became busier and busier,

and Mma Makutsi decided that the only thing to do, as Acting Manager, was to employ another mechanic for a few months, to see how things developed. She placed a small advertisement in the newspaper, and a man who had worked on the diamond mines as a diesel mechanic, but who had now retired, came forward and offered to work three days a week. He was started immediately, and he got on well with the apprentices.

"Mr J.L.B. Matekoni will like him," said Mma Ramotswe, "when he comes back and meets him."

"When will he come back?" asked Mma Makutsi. "It is over two weeks now."

"He'll be back one day," said Mma Ramotswe. "Let's not rush him."

That afternoon, she drove out to the orphan farm, parking her tiny white van directly outside Mma Potokwane's window. Mma Potokwane, who had seen her coming up the drive, had already put on the kettle by the time that Mma Ramotswe knocked at her door.

"Well, Mma Ramotswe," she said. "We have not seen you for a little while."

"I have been away," said Mma Ramotswe. "Then the rains came and the road out here has been very muddy. I did not want to get stuck in the mud."

"Very wise," said Mma Potokwane. "We had to get the bigger orphans out to push one or two trucks that got stuck just outside our drive. It was very difficult. All the orphans were covered in red mud and we had to hose them down in the yard."

"It looks like we will get good rains this year," said Mma Ramotswe. "That will be a very good thing for the country."

The kettle in the corner of the room began to hiss and Mma Potokwane arose to make tea.

"I have no cake to give you," she said. "I made a cake yesterday, but people have eaten every last crumb of it. It is as if the locusts had been here."

"People are very greedy," said Mma Ramotswe. "It would have been nice to have some cake. But I am not going to sit here and think about it."

They drank their tea in comfortable silence. Then Mma Ramotswe spoke.

"I thought I might take Mr J.L.B. Matekoni out for a run in the van," she ventured. "Do you think he might like that?"

Mma Potokwane smiled. "He would like it very much. He has been very quiet since he came here, but I have found out that there is something that he has been doing. I think it is a good sign."

"What is that?"

"He has been helping with that little boy," said Mma Potokwane. "You know the one that I asked you to find out something about? You remember that one?"

"Yes," said Mma Ramotswe, hesitantly. "I remember that little boy."

"Did you find out anything?" asked Mma Potokwane.

"No," said Mma Ramotswe. "I do not think that there is much that I can find out. But I do have an idea about that boy. It is just an idea."

Mma Potokwane slipped a further spoon of sugar into her tea and stirred it gently with a teaspoon.

"Oh yes? What's your idea?"

Mma Ramotswe frowned. "I do not think that my idea would help," she said. "In fact, I think it would not be helpful."

Mma Potokwane raised her teacup to her lips. She took a

long sip of tea and then replaced the cup carefully on the table.

"I think I know what you mean, Mma," she said. "I think that I have had the same idea. But I cannot believe it. Surely it cannot be true."

Mma Ramotswe shook her head. "That is what I have said to myself. People talk about these things, but they have never proved it, have they? They say that there are these wild children and that every so often somebody finds one. But do they ever actually prove that they have been brought up by animals? Is there any proof?"

"I have never heard of any," said Mma Potokwane.

"And if we told anybody what we think about this little boy, then what would happen? The newspapers would be full of it. There would be people coming from all over the world. They would probably try to take the boy off to live somewhere where they could look at him. They would take him outside Botswana."

"No," said Mma Potokwane. "The Government would never allow that."

"I don't know about that," said Mma Ramotswe. "They might. You can't be sure."

They sat silently. Then Mma Ramotswe spoke. "I think that there are some matters that are best left undisturbed," she said. "We don't want to know the answer to everything."

"I agree," said Mma Potokwane. "It is sometimes easier to be happy if you don't know everything."

Mma Ramotswe thought for a moment. It was an interesting proposition, and she was not sure if it was always true; it would require further thought, but not just then. She had a more immediate task in hand, and that was to drive Mr J.L.B. Matekoni out to Mochudi, where they could climb the kopje and look out over the plains. She was sure that he would like the sight of all that water; it would cheer him up.

"Mr J.L.B. Matekoni has been helping a bit with that boy," said Mma Potokwane. "It has been good for him to have something to do. I have seen him teaching him how to use a catapult. And I also hear that he has been teaching him words—teaching him how to speak. He is being very kind to him, and that, I think, is a good sign."

Mma Ramotswe smiled. She imagined Mr J.L.B. Matekoni teaching the wild boy the words for the things that he saw about him; teaching him the words for his world, the words for Africa.

MR J.L.B. Matekoni was not very communicative on the way up to Mochudi, sitting in the passenger seat of the tiny white van, staring out of the window at the unfolding plains and the other travellers on the road. He made a few remarks, though, and he even asked about what was happening at the garage, which he had not done at all when she had last gone to see him in his quiet room at the orphan farm.

"I hope that Mma Makutsi is controlling those apprentices of mine," he said. "They are such lazy boys. All they think about is women."

"There are still those problems with women," she said. "But she is making them work hard and they are doing well."

They reached the Mochudi turnoff and soon they were on the road that ran straight up towards the hospital, the kgotla, and the boulder-strewn kopje behind it.

"I think we should climb up the kopje," said Mma Ramotswe. "There is a good view from up there. We can see the difference that the rains have made."

"I am too tired to climb," said Mr J.L.B. Matekoni. "You go up. I shall stay down here."

"No," said Mma Ramotswe, firmly. "We shall both go up. You take my arm."

The climb did not take long, and soon they were standing on the edge of a large expanse of elevated rock, looking down on Mochudi: on the church, with its red tin roof, on the tiny hospital, where the heroic daily battle was fought, with small resources against such powerful enemies, and out, over the plains to the south. The river was flowing now, broadly and lazily, winding its way past clumps of trees and bush and the clusters of compounds that made up the straggling village. A small herd of cattle was being driven along a path near the river, and from where they stood the cattle looked tiny, like toys. But the wind was in their direction, and the sound of their bells could be made out, a distant, soft sound, so redolent of the Botswana bushland, so much the sound of home. Mma Ramotswe stood quite still; a woman on a rock in Africa, which was who, and where, she wanted to be.

"Look," said Mma Ramotswe. "Look down there. That is the house where I lived with my father. That is my place."

Mr J.L.B. Matekoni looked down and smiled. He smiled; and she noticed.

"I think you are feeling a bit better now, aren't you," she said.

Mr J.L.B. Matekoni nodded his head.

MORE FROM THE NO. 1 LADIES' DETECTIVE AGENCY

THE NO. 1 LADIES' DETECTIVE AGENCY

Millions of readers have fallen in love with the witty, wise Mma Ramotswe and her Botswana adventures. Share the magic of Alexander McCall Smith's No. 1 Ladies' Detective Agency series in two alternate editions:

1-4000-3477-9 (pbk)
0-375-42387-7 (hc)

TEARS OF THE GIRAFFE

The No. 1 Ladies' Detective Agency is growing, and in the midst of solving her usual cases—from an unscrupulous maid to a missing American—eminently sensible and cunning detective Mma Ramotswe ponders her impending marriage, promotes her talented secretary, and finds her family suddenly and unexpectedly increased by two.

Volume 2
1-4000-3135-4 (pbk)

MORALITY FOR BEAUTIFUL GIRLS

While trying to resolve some financial problems for her business, Mma Ramotswe finds herself investigating the alleged poisoning of a government official as well as the moral character of the four finalists of the Miss Beauty and Integrity contest. Other difficulties arise at her fiancé's Tlokweng Road Speedy Motors, as Mma Ramotswe discovers he is more complicated than he seems.

Volume 3
1-4000-3136-2 (pbk)

The mysteries are "smart and sassy . . . [with] the power to amuse or shock or touch the heart, sometimes all at once."
—*Los Angeles Times*

THE KALAHARI TYPING SCHOOL FOR MEN

Mma Precious Ramotswe is content. But, as always, there are troubles. Mr J.L.B. Matekoni has not set the date for their wedding, her assistant Mma Makutsi wants a husband, and worst of all, a rival detective agency has opened up in town. Of course, Precious will manage these things, as she always does, with her uncanny insight and good heart.

Volume 4
1-4000-3180-X (pbk)
0-375-42217-X (hc)

THE FULL CUPBOARD OF LIFE

Mma Ramotswe has weighty matters on her mind. She has been approached by a wealthy lady to check up on several suitors. Are these men interested in her or just her money? This may be difficult to find out, but it's just the kind of case Mma Ramotswe likes.

Volume 5
1-4000-3181-8 (pbk)
0-375-42218-8 (hc)

IN THE COMPANY OF CHEERFUL LADIES

Precious Ramotswe is busier than usual at the No. 1 Ladies' Detective Agency when the appearance of a strange intruder in her house and a mysterious pumpkin in her yard add to her concerns. But what finally rattles Mma Ramotswe's normally unshakable composure is the visitor who forces her to confront a painful secret from her past.

Volume 6
0-375-42271-4 (hc)
Paperback available Spring 2006

A New Series Begins

THE SUNDAY PHILOSOPHY CLUB

THE SUNDAY PHILOSOPHY CLUB

Isabel Dalhousie is fond of problems, and sometimes she becomes interested in problems that are, quite frankly, none of her business—including some that are best left to the police. Filled with endearingly thorny characters and a Scottish atmosphere as thick as a highland mist, *The Sunday Philosophy Club* is an irresistible pleasure.

Volume 1
1-4000-7709-5 (pbk)
0-375-42298-6 (hc)

FRIENDS, LOVERS, CHOCOLATE

While taking care of her niece Cat's delicatessen, Isabel meets a heart transplant patient who has had some strange experiences in the wake of surgery. Against the advice of her housekeeper, Isabel is intent on investigating. Matters are further complicated when Cat returns from vacation with a new boyfriend, and Isabel's fondness for him lands her in another muddle.

Volume 2
0-375-42299-4 (hc)
Paperback available Fall 2006

The Official Home of Alexander McCall Smith on the Web

WWW.ALEXANDERMCCALLSMITH.COM

A comprehensive Web site for new readers and longtime fans alike, with five exclusive content areas:

- **THE NO. 1 LADIES' DETECTIVE AGENCY**
  The original site for McCall Smith's bestselling series. Explore Precious Ramotswe's Botswana through book descriptions, a photo gallery, advice from Mma Ramotswe, and more.

- **THE SUNDAY PHILOSOPHY CLUB**
  Enter a Scottish atmosphere as thick as a highland mist, complete with a photo tour of Isabel Dalhousie's Edinburgh.

- **PROFESSOR DR VON IGELFELD ENTERTAINMENTS**
  Three original paperback novellas introducing the eccentric and ever-likable Professor Dr von Igelfeld, his colleagues, and their comic adventures.

- **ABOUT THE AUTHOR**
  Read about Alexander McCall Smith and get updates on tour events and other author activities.

- **JOIN THE COMMUNITY**
  Share the world of Alexander McCall Smith with friends, family, and fellow book club members. Print our free Reading Group Guides and sign up for the Alexander McCall Smith Fan Club and e-Newsletter.